HELP!
I'm Trapped...

W9-BNP-628

Volume One

TODD STRASSER

SCHOLASTIC INC.

New York Toronto London Auckland Sydney
Mexico City New Delhi Hong Kong Buenos Aires

Help! I'm Trapped in the First Day of School.
ISBN 0-590-48647-0, Copyright © 1994 by Todd Strasser.

Help! I'm Trapped in the First Day of Summer Camp.
ISBN 0-590-02965-7, Copyright © 1997 by Todd Strasser.

12 11 10 9 8 7 6 5 4 3 2 1   6 7 8 9 10/0

Printed in the U.S.A.   **40**

ISBN 0-439-81973-3

First Book Club printing, March 2006

Contents

HELP!

I'm Trapped in the First Day of School

To Leigh and Terry

1

DAY ONE

Beep . . . beep . . . beep! The alarm on the night table went off and I opened my eyes. I'd just had the weirdest dream about a groundhog named Bill. Why would I dream about a groundhog? I didn't have time to wonder about it. Today was the first day of school. As much as I hated going back, there was one thing I was looking forward to. This year Alex Silver and I were going to rule.

"Ready to conquer the world, Mr. Big Shot?" my sister Jessica asked when I came into the kitchen. She was sitting at the kitchen table, having a bowl of granola.

"Drop dead." I pulled out a new box of chocolate Pop-Tarts from the cupboard and tore it open.

Over the summer Jessica had changed from

1

being your average pain-in-the-butt big sister to being a super pain-in-the-butt PC big sister. PC stood for Politically Correct, which basically meant she had become a vegetarian, was into a million dumb causes, and always took the side of the underdog. She couldn't go anywhere without six different red, or maroon, or green ribbons pinned to her clothes, which were all black.

Today she was wearing a tight black leotard and a short black skirt. She'd also dyed her hair black and had her nose pierced with a small gold hoop.

To me, PC stood for Pea-brained Cretin.

"You're being really immature, you know," she said.

"Look who's talking," I replied as I put two Pop-Tarts in the toaster. "Just because you're going into tenth grade doesn't mean you're Miss Know-It-All."

"I know that Alex Silver is really bad news," Jessica said. "Ever since you got to know him, you've changed."

"I've changed?" I had to laugh. "Look at you. Every day you dress like you're going to a funeral. And what's the story with that nose ring? I mean, doesn't it get all crusty on the inside?"

"See?" Jessica said. "That's not Jake Sherman talking. That's Alex Silver. You started hanging around with him this summer and now you think being gross, mean, and disgusting makes you cool."

"Get lost." I really couldn't stand her moralizing.

"Whatever happened to Andy Kent and Josh Hopka?" Jessica asked.

"They're still around," I said. My Pop-Tarts popped out of the toaster.

"You never see them anymore."

"Because they're dorks, okay?"

"They used to be your best friends."

"Yeah, well, that was then and this is now." I picked up my Pop-Tarts and stood at the kitchen counter next to the window. Mom and Dad had already left for work.

"Look, Jake, I know the eighth-graders picked on you on your first day of sixth grade," Jessica said. "But that doesn't mean you have to pick on sixth-graders now that *you're* in eighth grade."

"Who said I was going to pick on anybody?" I asked defensively.

Jessica gave me a knowing look. "I heard you talking on the phone last night to Alex about calling yourselves the Knights of Wedgy and getting all the sixth-graders."

I turned and looked out the kitchen window so that Jessica wouldn't see the smile on my face. It was true. Alex and I planned to start the year by wedgying everyone in sight.

From our window I could see the bus stop at the corner of Magnolia Street and Bay Drive. A small kid with short blond hair and glasses was standing on the corner, looking around nervously as if he was worried he wasn't in the right place.

"Do you believe it?" I said. "The bus won't even be here for fifteen minutes and some kid's already waiting. He *has* to be a sixth-grader."

"I remember *you* got to the bus stop early on your first day of middle school, too," Jessica said as she cleared her bowl from the table.

"Did not," I said.

"Did too." Jessica put her dish in the sink and squinted out the window. "I've never seen him before. Must be new."

First victim, I thought, smiling to myself. Out of the corner of my eye, I noticed that Jessica was staring at me.

"Jake . . ." she said in a warning tone.

"What?" I asked innocently.

"I know what you're thinking. You really ought to grow up."

"You mean, wear a ring in my nose and dress like an undertaker?" I asked.

Jessica gritted her teeth and made a fist. I could tell I'd made her really mad.

Suddenly in the background, the town's fire siren went off — *Whaaaaa-O-Whaaaaa-O-Whaaaa!* — alerting the volunteer firemen of a fire.

4

A moment later it was followed by the sound of a car honking in our driveway.

"That's Cathy," Jessica said. "Her sister's giving us a ride to school. Want to come?"

"No way," I said. "I'm meeting Alex at the bus stop."

"Of course." My sister sneered. "You're Sir Jake, a Knight of Wedgy now. It's time to start your little reign of terror."

2

Outside it was still summery. The trees were green and insects buzzed around in the warm air. As I walked down to the bus stop, I couldn't help feeling good. Today me and Alex were finally on the top of the heap.

Eeeeiiiiirrrrnnnn! Eeeeiiiiirrrrnnnn! A big red-and-silver pumper truck raced down Bay Drive with its lights flashing. A couple of seconds later another fire truck shot past. It looked like they were heading a few blocks away. I didn't think much of it. Most of the time it just turned out to be a false alarm.

By now Alex had arrived at the bus stop, along with half a dozen other kids. Alex was sporting a new buzz cut and a diamond stud earring. He was wearing a black T-shirt, jeans, and cool boots.

When he saw me, he raised his hand. "Sir Jake, dude!"

"Sir Alex, bud!" We gave each other high fives and glanced around at the other kids, who looked back at us nervously. For the first time in our lives, we were the biggest kids at the bus stop.

"Are we the Knights of Wedgy?" Alex asked loudly enough for everyone to hear.

"Yes!" I said.

"Are we bad?" Alex asked with a grin.

"Yes!"

"Do we wedgy?"

"Most righteously, yes!"

Slap! We gave each other another high five. Then Alex turned to the little group around us. "Everyone will now stand shoulder-to-shoulder at attention," he ordered.

"What if we don't?" asked Robbie Bayuk, a seventh-grade wise guy.

"You'll be wedgied by royal order of the king," Alex threatened.

Robbie quickly got into line with the others. The only one who didn't get into line was the new blond kid with the glasses. He was wearing a blue short-sleeve shirt and neatly pressed khaki slacks and was carrying a new light-green backpack.

Alex peered down at him and rubbed his chin. "Sir Jake," he called to me. "What manner of creature is this?"

"Why, I believe it's a dweeb, Sir Alex," I replied.

Alex nodded. "Tell me, dweeb, have you trouble hearing?"

The kid shook his head.

"Then why aren't you standing with the others?"

"Uh, well, I was just wondering what a wedgy was?"

The kids in line all snickered. Alex stepped closer, and the kid stepped back, frightened.

"Do my ears deceive me?" Alex asked. "Truly have you no idea what a wedgy is?"

The kid shook his head.

Alex looked over at me. "Tell me, Sir Jake, what thinketh you of this?"

"I thinketh we must learn this dweeb's name," I replied. "And from what strange wedgiless land he has come."

"What is your name, dweeb?" Alex asked.

"Uh, Oliver," the kid stammered. "But everyone calls me Ollie."

"Ollie?" Alex repeated in disbelief.

"Be that a dorkish name or what?" I asked.

"It's . . . it's not like I had a choice," Ollie replied in a quavering voice.

"And from what strange wedgiless land do you come, Dweeb Ollie?" Alex asked.

"Uh, Ohio," Ollie said. "Near Cleveland."

"And have they no wedgies near Cleveland, Dweeb Ollie of Ohio?" I asked.

"Not where I come from," Ollie said.

"Tell us, Dweeb Ollie of Ohio," said Alex. "Who picks out your clothes for you?"

"Uh, my mom."

"Is this not cute?" I grinned. "His mommy still dresses him in the morning."

"And you really don't know what a wedgy is?" Alex asked.

Ollie shook his head. Alex and I exchanged a serious look.

"You know what this means, Sir Jake?" Alex said.

"Death?" I guessed.

"Next time," Alex said. "But for now, he must run around the block."

"Now?" Ollie's jaw dropped.

"Forsooth." Alex nodded.

"But I'll miss the bus," Ollie said.

"Not if you hurry."

"But . . ." Ollie whimpered.

Alex bent down and hooked his fingers through the bottom laces of Ollie's brand-new white tennis shoes. Then he pulled hard, tightening the laces all the way up.

"Ow!" Ollie cried and stepped back.

"Dost thou know what that was, Dweeb Ollie of Ohio?" Alex asked, straightening up.

Ollie shook his head.

"A mere shoe wedgy," Alex informed him. "And nothing compared to what will happen next if you do not get your butt in motion."

Ollie started to back away.

"*Now!*" Alex shouted.

Ollie took off down the sidewalk. I figured he'd get back in time to catch the bus.

"Like a true dweeb." Alex crossed his arms and turned to me. "Hast thou any gum, Sir Jake?"

"Why, yes, Sir Alex." I pulled a pack of Juicy Fruit out of my T-shirt pocket and gave him a stick. Meanwhile, across the street, Mr. Mac-Dowell came out of his house. He was an old guy with thin white hair. We watched him walk stiffly to his garage.

"Observe this," Alex said, going across the street. While the old man went into his garage and got into his car, Alex moved one of Mr. MacDowell's garbage cans into his driveway. Then he came back across the street.

A few seconds later Mr. MacDowell backed his car down the driveway.

Crunck! As the car reached the curb, it hit the garbage can, knocking it over and spilling out white garbage bags.

Muttering to himself, Mr. MacDowell slowly got out of his car.

"Clap," Alex ordered the sixth- and seventh-graders.

No one clapped.

"I said *clap!*" Alex snarled.

The kids started clapping. Across the street Mr. MacDowell winced as he bent down and put the garbage bags back in the can. Then he straightened up and pointed a bony finger at us.

"It's not funny!" he said angrily. "You kids ought to show some respect."

Just then the school bus turned the corner and stopped.

"What about the new kid?" Robbie Bayuk asked.

We looked down the block. There was no sign of Ollie.

"Me thinks he shall have to learn to run faster," Alex said with a shrug, and climbed on.

I hesitated, sort of hoping Ollie would sprint around the corner. After all, it was the kid's first day. Did he really have to miss the bus?

3

Exercising our eighth-grade privileges, the Knights of Wedgy kicked all the younger kids out of the back of the bus and sat down. At school we found our new lockers.

"Cool, Sir Alex, we are almost next to each other," I said as we stood at our lockers. We both took out the letters we'd gotten over the summer with our new combinations.

Brinnnggg! The homeroom bell rang. Alex and I were just about to go in when we heard rapid footsteps coming down the hall toward us. We turned and saw who it was.

"Why, it's Dweeb Ollie of Ohio," Alex said with a nasty grin. "You have arrived!"

Ollie's face was red and he was breathing so hard that he couldn't talk.

"Is it possible that Dweeb Ollie of Ohio ran all the way to school?" Alex asked.

Ollie nodded and gasped. "I . . . I can't find my homeroom."

"And what room might that be, Ollie boy?" Alex asked, giving me a wink.

"One-oh-six."

Alex gave him an awestruck look. "Forsooth! You must travel all the way to the other side of school. Take the stairs at the end of this hall. When you get up to the second floor, turn right and go all the way to the end of that hall. Then make another right and go to the end of *that* hall. Your destination will be right around there."

"I go up the stairs, then right down the first hall, right down the second and I'm there?" Ollie repeated.

"That is correct," Alex said. "But you must hurry, Dweeb Ollie of Ohio. You must not be late for homeroom on your first day."

Ollie took off and ran all the way down the hall and up the stairs. As soon as he was out of sight, I cracked up. Room 106 was only two doors away!

"He'll never find it now!" Alex cried, giving me a high five. "He'll probably be lost until lunch!"

I had to admit that it was kind of funny. Besides, Ollie wouldn't get into trouble. Everyone expected sixth-graders to get lost on the first day of school. Still laughing, Alex and I went into homeroom.

"Hello, boys," someone said.

We turned and found Ms. Rogers, who'd started as a new teacher when we were in sixth grade.

She had black, wavy hair and big, blue eyes and used to call me her favorite troublemaker.

"Hey, Ms. Rogers, how was your summer?" I asked.

"Wonderful, Jake," she said, showing off a gold wedding band on her ring finger. "Look what I just got."

"You mean . . .?" My jaw dropped.

Ms. Rogers smiled and nodded. "Mr. Dirksen and I finally tied the knot."

"Wow, congratulations," I said, noticing that Alex was giving me a funny look.

"Does that mean now we have to call you Mrs. *Dork*sen?" Alex asked.

The smile disappeared from Ms. Rogers's face. "No, we decided I'd still use my maiden name. Now go find your seats, boys."

We went to the back of the room and sat. The seat next to me was empty. Alex slouched way down in his chair.

"How come you're so friendly to her?" he whispered while Ms. Rogers took attendance.

"I don't know," I whispered back. "Guess I've always thought she was okay."

"A teacher!" Alex wrinkled his nose as if it were impossible for any teacher to be okay.

"Jake Sherman?" Ms. Rogers called.

"Here." I raised my hand.

"Alex Silver?"

Alex gave her a cool little half-wave.

"Amber Sweeny?" Ms. Rogers called.

No one answered.

"Ever heard of her?" Alex whispered.

"She must be new," I whispered back.

Ms. Rogers finished taking attendance and picked up a blue sheet of paper. "Principal Blanco has asked all the homeroom teachers to read this bulletin," she said, clearing her throat. " 'Hello, and welcome back to school. We here at the Burt Itchupt Middle School hope that you all had a wonderful summer and that you're ready to buckle down for a really exciting year of school — ' "

"Really exciting?" muttered Alex. A couple of kids around us giggled.

"Ahem." Ms. Rogers cleared her throat again and continued. " 'Every year we welcome a new group of sixth-graders, and this year is no exception. We ask that all seventh- and eighth-graders show our new students the courtesy and respect we are accustomed to here at Burt Itchupt.' "

"Burp It Up," Alex whispered, and the kids chuckled.

Ms. Rogers stopped reading and gave him the evil eye. "That's enough, Alex."

Alex grinned at everyone. I guess he liked the attention. Then he raised his hand. "Uh, Ms. Rogers, I'm not sure I understand what you mean by courtesy and respect."

"Well," Ms. Rogers replied. "In your case, Alex, that would mean don't give them incorrect directions, don't jam their lockers, don't make them sing, or force them into the bathroom used by the opposite sex."

Alex raised his hand again. "What about wedgies?"

"I would imagine that any student caught giving wedgies will be immediately suspended from school."

"Would that include nature wedgies?" Alex asked.

The class tittered.

"What is a nature wedgy?" Ms. Rogers asked.

"It's like a regular wedgy, except you throw in rocks and pinecones and burrs and stuff."

"Ew!" "Gross!" "Give me a break!" All around the classroom kids made disgusted sounds.

"I would think that anyone caught giving a nature wedgy would be subject to the harshest punishment Mr. Blanco could issue," Ms. Rogers replied.

Alex raised his hand again.

"Now what, Alex?" Ms. Rogers asked.

"What about a Melvin?"

More chuckles spread through the room.

Ms. Rogers gave him a blank look.

"It's a wedgy from the front," Alex explained.

"Ugh!" the guys in the room groaned. Just the thought of it was enough to make you ill.

"No Melvins," said Ms. Rogers firmly.

Then the door opened and a girl stepped into

the classroom. She had long straight-brown hair, almond-shaped green eyes, and smooth flawless skin. She bit the corner of her lip nervously.

"*Hubba hubba!*" Alex whispered under his breath.

"Can I help you?" Ms. Rogers asked the girl.

"Is this Ms. Rogers's homeroom?" she asked in a soft voice.

"Are you Amber Sweeny?" Ms. Rogers asked. The girl nodded.

"*I'm in love!*" Alex groaned and the kids around him chuckled.

"Please take a seat," Ms. Rogers said. "I was just reading a bulletin from Principal Blanco regarding treatment of the new sixth-graders, but I don't think it's something you'll need to worry about."

Amber Sweeny smiled slightly and quickly took a seat . . . right next to me.

For a moment the class was totally silent. I glanced around the room and saw that almost everyone was staring at Amber with the same starstruck expression.

As if a goddess had just entered our midst.

Then I felt someone poke me in the ribs. It was Alex.

"Say something to her," he whispered, just loud enough for the kids around us to hear.

"Get lost," I whispered back.

"Chicken?" he taunted.

I felt my face turn red, but didn't say anything. I was pretty sure Amber could hear Alex, too.

"*Bawk, bawk, bawk,*" Alex started to make chicken sounds. The kids around us started to giggle.

"*You* say something to her," I whispered back.

"I would, but I'm not sitting next to her," Alex replied.

"Jake, what's going on back there?" Ms. Rogers asked.

I quickly turned around and faced the front. The kids around us were still giggling. I grinned nervously and felt my face turn even redder.

"Uh, nothing, Ms. Rogers," I said.

Brinnggg . . . The bell rang and it was time to go to our first class. Everyone got up. I could feel Ms. Rogers's eyes on me as I headed for the door.

"Jake?" she said, just as I was about to leave the room.

"Uh, yeah?" I paused.

"I'd like to have a word with you."

The other kids gave me looks and smirked.

"But I'll be late for my next class," I said.

"I can give you a pass," Ms. Rogers said. "I'm a teacher, remember? Or maybe you've forgotten."

It was obvious from her tone that she was mad. Alex came by and patted me on the shoulder.

"Catch you later, Sir Jake," he said quietly and went out, leaving me to face Ms. Rogers alone.

18

4

Ms. Rogers leaned against her desk with her arms crossed.

"Something's changed," she said.

I tried to imagine what Alex would say. Probably something cool like, "Oh, yeah?" or "Tell me about it." But somehow, I couldn't quite get myself to say anything like that.

"Do you know what it is?" Ms. Rogers asked.

I had a feeling I knew, but I shook my head anyway.

"It's you," she said. "And do you know what about you has changed?"

"Uh, I got a little taller over the summer?"

Ms. Rogers shook her head.

"Well, uh, I've noticed a couple of whiskers on my upper lip," I said.

Ms. Rogers smiled slightly. "No, Jake. What's changed is that you're starting to get into trouble again. Remember in sixth grade when I used to call you my favorite troublemaker?"

I nodded.

"Well, what seemed cute and funny then doesn't seem so cute and funny now," she said. "You're two years older and it's time to grow up."

I looked down at the floor. She was starting to sound like my sister and my parents.

"May I give you a word of advice?" Ms. Rogers asked.

I shrugged.

"Find a new friend."

The rest of the morning was the typical first-day stuff: information about fire drills, lectures on good behavior and respecting each other, explanations of grading procedures, and so on.

The high point of the morning was gym. Mr. Cooper, the gym teacher, said we had to wash ourselves and our gym uniforms frequently because our body chemistry was changing in ways that teachers and other students might find offensive.

"Tell me, Sir Jake," said Alex after gym, as we walked to lunch. "Hast thou ever heard a more original way of saying we had B-O?"

"Forsooth, I have not," I replied with a grin.

We walked into the cafeteria. The lunch line was pretty long, so we cut in front.

"Hey, what d'ya think you're doing?" a kid behind us asked.

"Exercising our eighth-grade privileges, peasant," Alex replied.

"That's not allowed," the kid said. "I'm gonna tell Principal Blanco."

"So be it," Alex said with a shrug.

The kid turned to go, but another kid grabbed his arm. "I wouldn't if I were you."

"Why not?" asked the first kid.

"They'll make sure you pay for the rest of the year," the other kid said.

"But it's not fair," complained the first kid.

"Don't worry," said the other kid. "You'll get your chance when you're in eighth grade."

Alex and I smiled at each other as we slid our trays down the silver railing toward the lunch ladies. It felt good to be on the top of the heap. It felt good to be feared.

The menu for the first day was always cheeseburgers and fries. It was a Burp-It-Up tradition. Moments later we came out of the lunch line with our trays and looked around for a table.

"Check it out, Sir Jake." Alex nodded toward Amber Sweeny, who sat alone eating a salad. "Dost thou think Princess Amber would like company?"

"Certainly, Sir Alex, go right ahead," I replied.

"Well, I meant . . ." Alex hesitated. "We could go together."

"Well, uh . . ." The idea of sitting with her

21

made me pretty nervous. I had the feeling Alex was nervous about it, too. Just then Ms. Rogers, who was on lunch duty, stopped by the table where Amber was sitting and started to chat with her.

"Too late," Alex muttered. "The evil witch has foiled our plans."

"Perhaps tomorrow we will sit with the princess," I suggested.

"Yes, tomorrow," Alex agreed.

We headed toward an empty table. Out of the corner of my eye I noticed two other kids heading for it, too. We all got there at the same time and put our trays down. Looking up, I saw that the other two guys were my old friends, Andy Kent and Josh Hopka.

It looked like Andy had gotten a little taller over the summer and had cut his black hair short. Josh had thinned down a little. His face was tan and full of freckles.

We all nodded at each other and sat down. I sat across from Alex, and Andy sat across from Josh. I could feel their eyes on me.

"So how was your summer, Jake?" Josh asked.

"Okay," I said, picking up a soggy fry and biting into it. "How was yours?"

"Okay," Josh said. "Didn't see you around much."

"Yeah." What else could I do but nod?

Josh turned back to Andy. "Guess Jake's got a new friend," he said loudly.

"Yeah, so he doesn't need his old friends anymore," Andy replied, picking up his burger.

"I hear they call themselves the Knights of Wedgy," Josh said. "The word is they did a real number on some new kid this morning."

Alex bristled. "Are these guys bothering you?" he asked me loudly.

"No." I quickly shook my head. The last thing I wanted to do was get into a fight with my old friends. Actually, I was kind of surprised that they were so peeved about not seeing me over the summer.

Meanwhile, Andy took a big bite of his cheeseburger and started to chew.

"*Blech!*" Without warning he bent over and spit the cheeseburger back onto his tray.

"Gross!" Alex shouted, jumping up from the table.

"What happened?" I asked.

"I think he hurled," said Alex.

"I didn't hurl," Andy said, wiping his mouth with a napkin. He pointed at the half-chewed yellow-and-brown glob on the tray. "That's the worst thing I ever tasted."

"Well, cover it up or something," Josh said. "I'm getting sick just looking at it."

Andy took the bun from his cheeseburger and

covered the glob. "Forget it. I just lost my appetite."

Alex and I looked at each other. Andy may have lost his appetite, but we still had ours. We sat down again and picked up our cheeseburgers, but neither of us took a bite.

"You go first," Alex said.

"No, *you*," I said.

"I dare you."

"Drop dead."

"He will if he eats that thing," Andy said. "I swear, it tastes like it was left over from last year."

"I'll do it if you'll do it," Alex dared me.

"Promise?" I asked.

"You guys are nuts," said Andy.

"Maybe it was just *your* burger, Andy," Josh said.

Alex and I brought the cheeseburgers up to our noses and sniffed them. Alex wrinkled his nose.

"How does it smell?" Josh asked.

"Like regular mystery meat to me," I said.

"They must have put something on it to mask the smell," Andy said. "I'm warning you, guys, you eat that thing and the only way you'll leave this cafeteria is by Medivac."

My stomach growled hungrily. I knew if I was hungry, Alex and Josh were hungry, too.

"What do you think?" Alex asked.

"Maybe Josh is right and Andy's was the only bad one," I said.

"I say we all bite at once," Alex said.

Josh and I glanced at each other and nodded. We all slowly opened our mouths and put the cheeseburgers in, but none of us bit.

"Guffaffed, buff." Josh tried to talk with the cheeseburger bun in his mouth.

I turned to Andy. *"Whuff fee fay?"* I asked with my bun still in my mouth.

"I think he said, go ahead, bite," Andy said.

I turned to Alex. *"Whuff afout yoo?"*

"What about you?" Andy interpreted.

"I fill fen yoof foo," Alex replied.

"He says he will when you do," Andy said.

"Fofay," I said. *"Uh fun, an uh foo, and uh fee!"* Josh and I both bit down at the same time.

"Blech!" The horrible taste of spoiled meat filled my mouth. Josh and I spit out our bites.

"That's the worst!" I cried.

"It's rancid!" Josh quickly sipped his orange drink to get rid of the taste.

"You dorks!" Alex laughed and put down his untouched burger.

"Hey!" Josh said angrily. "We all agreed to bite at the same time. It was your idea."

"Give me a break," Alex said with a big smile.

Josh picked up his tray. "Come on, Andy, let's get something else to eat." He and Andy got up.

Josh looked back at me. "Great friend, Jake," he said sarcastically.

Alex and I watched them leave.

"You really used to hang out with those two?" he asked.

I nodded.

Alex shook his head. "Chumps."

5

We ate potato chips and ice cream for lunch and then kicked the seventh-graders off the basketball court and played H-O-R-S-E until the bell.

Next class was science with Mr. Dirksen, who we'd last had in sixth grade. We used to call him Mr. *Dork*sen, but after he and I accidentally switched bodies, he'd become a much cooler teacher.

As we walked into the classroom, I saw that Andy and Josh had just arrived. Mr. Dirksen was standing at the blackboard writing something. Only, he didn't look like Mr. Dirksen anymore.

"Whoa! Mr. Dirksen, you got hair!" Andy cried.

Mr. Dirksen ran his hand over his his head, which used to be bald, but now had straight brown hair.

"Had a transplant," he said. "What do you think?"

"Did Ms. Rogers make you do it?" Josh asked.

"She said she didn't care either way," Mr. Dirksen said, "but secretly I think she likes it."

Brinnnggg. . . . The bell rang.

"All right, everyone," Mr. Dirksen said, handing out double sheets of paper. "Take your seats. Hurry, we have lots to do."

Alex and I sat down in the back of the room. Josh and Andy sat in the front. Mr. Dirksen started to close the door when Amber Sweeny hurried in.

"Sorry I'm late," she said breathlessly.

"Just find a seat," Mr. Dirksen said.

There was an empty seat next to me, and Amber sat down in it. She gave me a brief smile, and I smiled back nervously.

I felt a finger poke me in the ribs. "Now's your chance," Alex whispered.

"Chill, dude," I whispered back.

Meanwhile in front, Andy held up the pages Mr. Dirksen had just given out. "Uh, excuse me, but this looks an awful lot like a test."

"It is," Mr. Dirksen replied.

"What?" "Huh?" "Is he serious?" All around the room kids expressed their disbelief. I looked down at the test, which had something to do with naming the parts of a cell. Amber turned and gave me a puzzled look. It was the perfect chance to say something to her, but the words seemed to get caught in my throat.

"You can't give us a test on the first day of school," said Josh.

"Why not?" Mr. Dirksen asked.

"Because no one's had time to study," Andy said.

"A test is supposed to measure your knowledge in a certain area," Mr. Dirksen replied calmly. "I simply want to see how much you know."

"Great," Andy groaned. "So we'll all start off the year with an F."

"On the contrary," Mr. Dirksen said. "You'll start off the year with a good idea of what you're going to study."

"But it's not fair," said a girl named Julia Sax.

"What isn't fair about it?" Mr. Dirksen replied.

"We had no advance warning," said Julia.

"Yeah, this is really gonna mess up our GPAs," said Josh.

"It won't harm your grade point averages at all," said Mr. Dirksen.

"It won't?" Andy frowned.

"I'll grade it, but it's not going to count," Mr. Dirksen said with a big smile.

All around the room kids let out big sighs of relief.

"Why didn't you tell us that in the first place?" Andy asked.

"No one gave me a chance to," Mr. Dirksen explained.

Everybody had a big laugh, and then we spent the rest of the period trying to do the test. After class, Alex and I stopped at our lockers to dump some books.

"What a jerk," Alex said.

"Who?" I said.

"Mr. Dirksen."

"Why?" I said, surprised. "He said the test wouldn't count."

"Yeah." Alex nodded. "That's what he *said*, but you'll see."

Just then Amber Sweeny walked by and went down the hall.

"You had the perfect chance to talk to her," Alex said.

"What was I supposed to say?" I asked, closing my locker.

"You could have said a million things," Alex said. "Like what a jerk Mr. Dirksen was. Or how hot-looking she is. Or just about anything."

"I didn't see you say anything to her," I said as we started down the hall.

"I wasn't sitting next to her," said Alex. Then he added, "Hey, look who's coming."

Down the hall I caught a glimpse of a familiar-looking blond head being jostled in the crowd. A moment later we came face-to-face with Ollie. He stared up at us through his glasses.

"Why it's Dweeb Ollie of Ohio," Alex said with

a sinister grin. "You get to homeroom on time this morning?"

Ollie shook his head. "You got me really lost."

"Aw, isn't that too bad?" Alex pouted.

"I don't want to be late for my next class." Ollie started around Alex.

"Not so fast, Dweeb Ollie." Alex grabbed the strap of his backpack and stopped him. Then he looked at me. "Any teachers?"

I quickly looked up and down the hall. All I saw were kids. "Nope."

"Excellent." Alex started to tug Ollie. "It's very important that you learn about our school, Dweeb Ollie of Ohio. And one place you must get to know is . . . the girls' room."

"Oh, no!" Ollie gasped and tried to squirm out of Alex's grip. But Alex kicked the girls' room door open with his foot and pushed Ollie inside.

"Hey! Let me out!" Ollie's muffled shouts came through the wooden door. Alex held the door closed while I watched for teachers.

Thunk! Thunk! Thunk! Ollie pounded desperately on the inside of the girls' room door. "Come on, guys! Let me out! *Please!*"

Out in the hall, Alex smiled fiendishly as a bunch of kids stopped to see what the commotion was about.

"What's going on?" someone asked.

"I think he's got some kid trapped in the girls' room," said someone else.

Suddenly another voice joined Ollie's inside the girls' room. "Let him out, for Pete's sake."

It was a girl's voice. Alex quickly let go of the door. It swung open, and Ollie hurried out and sped down the hall without even looking at us. Alex and I nudged each other and chuckled.

Then Amber Sweeny stepped out of the girls' room.

Alex and I stopped smiling.

The crowd around us grew quiet.

Amber fixed us with her piercing green eyes.

"Grow up," she said, and walked away.

6

My parents usually didn't get home until around 7:30, so Jessica cooked dinner every night.

"How was school, Mr. Big Shot?" she asked that night as she dumped a package of spaghetti into a pot of water boiling on the stove.

"Okay." I sat slumped at the kitchen table. The memory of Amber's put-down was still ringing painfully in my ears.

"How many sixth-graders did you wedgy?" she asked.

I blinked as I realized that besides the shoe-wedgy of Dweeb Ollie of Ohio that morning, we hadn't wedgied anyone. "Uh, none."

Jessica looked surprised. "What happened to all your plans?"

"We did most of 'em," I said.

"Boy, you must've felt like big, tough eighth-graders pushing all those little kids around," Jessica said snidely.

"Look, just drop it, okay?"

Jessica shrugged and started to heat up the tomato sauce. Being a vegetarian, she never put any meat in it. "Remember that fire this morning?"

"Huh?" It took me a second to remember. "Oh, yeah, what about it?"

"It was a few blocks over," she said. "A new family just moved in. I heard they left the toaster oven on. There's hardly anything left."

"Wow, cool," I said. "Want to go over there after dinner and take a look?"

"I can't," Jessica said. "I have to read a whole chapter of biology, plus do geometry and world history."

"Too bad."

My sister gave me a look of utter disgust. "What's happened to you?"

"I don't know, what?" I asked, bewildered.

"When did you become to kind of the person who thinks it's cool when someone's house burns down?"

7

DAY TWO

*B*eep . . . *beep* . . . *beep!* The alarm went off and I opened my eyes. It was time to get up and go to school.

Jessica was in the kitchen having her usual bowl of granola when I came in.

"Ready?" she asked as I got the box of Pop-Tarts out of the cupboard.

"For what?" I asked, tearing the box open.

"It's the first day of school, remember?"

"What are you talking about?"I asked.

Jessica rolled her eyes. "Get a grip, Jake."

"*You* get a grip," I said. "The first day was yesterday."

Jessica stared at me like I was crazy. "I went to the pool with Cathy yesterday."

I stared back at Jessica like *she* was crazy. Then I looked down at the box of chocolate Pop-Tarts.

Why was I tearing open a new box? I'd just opened one yesterday. I looked in the cupboard for the open box, but it wasn't there.

"Hey, what'd you do with my Pop-Tarts?" I asked.

"They're in your hand."

"Not these," I said. "I opened a box yesterday. Where are they?"

"Don't look at me," my sister said. "I didn't touch them."

"Yeah, right." I didn't believe her. Then I noticed something else strange. "Why are you wearing the same clothes as yesterday?"

"What?" Jessica scowled at me.

"That's what you wore to school yesterday," I said. "Aren't you worried some of your politically correct friends might object?"

Jessica stared at me again like I was crazy. "Are you feeling okay?"

"I was until now," I said. "I mean, when you were in eighth grade, didn't Mr. Cooper give you that dumb lecture about how your body chemistry was changing in ways that teachers and other students might find offensive?"

"Yes," said my sister. "How did you know about that?"

"Because he gave it yesterday."

"He couldn't have, Jake. There was no school yesterday."

"Of course there was," I said. "You wore those clothes."

"I just got this top at the mall last night," Jessica said. "What's with you?"

"What's with me?" I asked. "Hey, I'm not the one pretending today's the first day of school."

"It *is* the first day."

Suddenly I figured out what she was up to. "Very funny, Jessica. Good joke."

"It's not a joke," my sister said. "I don't know what you're talking about."

"Yeah, right." The conversation was getting nowhere. I turned and looked out the kitchen window. Ollie was already at the bus stop.

"Do you believe it?" I said. "Dweeb Ollie's early again."

"Who?" Jessica asked.

"Ollie," I said. "Remember yesterday morning? That blond kid who got to the bus stop early? Well, his name's Oliver, but Alex dubbed him Dweeb Ollie of Ohio."

Jessica didn't answer. She just stared at me like I was completely out of my gourd.

"Oh, right," I said with a smile. "Now you don't remember *him* either."

Suddenly the town's fire siren began to blast — *Whaaaaa-O-Whaaaaa-O-Whaaaaa!* . . .

That's strange, I thought. *Two mornings in a row?*

A moment later a car horn honked.

"That's Cathy," Jessica said. "Her sister's giving us a ride to school. Want to come?"

Suddenly I felt a very weird sensation. Like major *déjà vu*. Weren't those the exact same words my sister had used the day before?

"Jake?"

"Huh?" I looked at her, puzzled.

"Are you okay?"

"Uh, yeah, sure."

"Cathy's sister's giving us a ride to school. You can come if you want."

"Uh, that's okay," I said. "I told Alex I'd meet him at the bus stop."

"Of course." Jessica smiled snidely as she left. "You're Sir Jake, a Knight of Wedgy now. It's time to start your little reign of terror."

A few moments later I left the house, feeling kind of weird.

Eeeeiiiirrrrnnnn! Eeeeiiiirrrrnnnn! The big red-and-silver pumper truck raced past, going down Bay Drive with its lights flashing. A couple of seconds later another fire truck shot past. Once again it looked like they were heading for a house a couple of blocks away.

That strange feeling grew stronger. Almost like it was yesterday all over again.

By the time I got to the bus stop, Alex and the

other kids had also arrived. Once again, Alex was wearing a black T-shirt.

When he saw me, he raised his hand. "Sir Jake, dude!"

I just stared at him. *What was going on?*

Alex frowned. "I said, Sir Jake, dude!"

I gave him the high five and glanced around at the other kids. They were all giving us the same scared looks and wearing the same clothes as the day before!

"Are we the Knights of Wedgy?" Alex asked.

"Yeah, sure," I said and turned to Ollie. Once again he gave me that awestruck, wide-eyed look. He was wearing the same blue short-sleeve shirt and khaki slacks as yesterday.

"Remember me?" I asked.

Ollie shook his head.

"Come on, Ollie," I said. "Me and Alex made you miss the bus yesterday. Then we got you lost at school and pushed you into the girls' room."

Ollie looked at me like I was crazy. "There was no school yesterday. And how do you know my name?"

"Yeah, what's with you, Jake?" Alex asked.

They were all staring at me — the same way Jessica had.

"Uh, nothing," I said.

"Good," Alex said. "Are we bad?"

I nodded.

"Do we wedgy?"

Again I nodded. Something totally bizarre was going on. Just as he had the day before, Alex turned to the little group around us and told them to stand at attention.

"What if we don't?" Robbie Bayuk asked again.

"You'll get wedgied," Alex threatened again.

"Wait a minute," I said. "Didn't anybody here go to school yesterday?"

Alex turned and gave me a peculiar look. "Why?"

"Because it was the — " I started to say "the first day of school," but then I caught myself. I knew they'd all gone to school the day before. I'd *seen* them go to school.

Everyone except Ollie got in the row.

Alex peered down at him. "What manner of creature is this?"

It *had* to be some kind of joke.

Alex turned to me. "Sir Jake, I asked you what manner of creature is this."

"It's a Dweeb Ollie of Ohio," I said. "You know that from yesterday."

Alex frowned. Then he turned to Ollie. "What's your name?"

"Well, my name's Oliver and I *am* from Ohio," the kid said. "And people do call me Ollie."

Alex looked back at me and grinned. "Very good, mind reader."

I didn't know what to say. This was impossible.

It couldn't be happening. And yet it was. Right before my eyes, everything was happening just as it had the day before. I listened in amazement as Ollie said he didn't know what a wedgy was. Then, just like the day before, Alex gave him a shoe wedgy and sent him around the block.

"Like a true dweeb," Alex muttered. Then he turned to me. "Hast thou any gum, Sir Jake?"

Gum? I'd had a pack yesterday, but I'd finished it at school.

"Sorry." I shook my head.

Alex frowned and stuck his hand into the pocket of my T-shirt. "What's this?" He pulled out a pack of Juicy Fruit.

"Uh . . ." I was sure I'd finished it the day before.

Alex pulled a stick out and put the pack back into my pocket. "I am surprised at you, Sir Jake. We Knights of Wedgy share everything."

I knew for a fact that I'd finished that gum the day before. Now I watched in total amazement as Alex went across the street and moved Mr. MacDowell's garbage can into the driveway again. Mr. MacDowell backed into it, and Alex made the kids clap.

Something totally and extremely weird was going on. The day before was all happening all over again! And no one seemed to know it except me!

8

At school I did my combination and opened my locker. The afternoon before, I'd left some books in it. But now it was completely empty.

"Uh, Sir Jake?"

I turned and found Alex holding the letter his locker combination had come on.

"You just did your combination without looking at your letter," he said.

"Oh, uh, yeah," I stammered.

Alex squinted at me. "You *memorized* it?"

"Uh, I guess."

"Listen, Sir Jake," Alex said, stepping close and speaking in a low voice. "Only dorks memorize their locker combination before the first day of school. Now I'm willing to pretend it didn't happen, but get real, dude."

Brinnnggg! The homeroom bell rang. Alex and I were just about to go in when we heard the sound of rapid footsteps coming down the hall toward us. It was Ollie, red-faced and out of breath.

Once again he couldn't find his homeroom. Once again Alex winked at me and sent him on a wild-goose chase. Then we went into our homeroom.

I think I was in a daze while Ms. Rogers read the bulletin from Principal Blanco. Every single person was wearing exactly what they'd worn the day before. And nobody complained that she'd read the bulletin yesterday.

What did it mean? Why was it happening?

Once again Alex made his wisecracks, and asked about nature wedgies and Melvins.

Then the door opened and Amber Sweeny came in, and everyone stared at her with the same star-struck expression. Alex made the same wise-cracks. Then the kids around us chuckled, and I felt him poke me in the ribs.

"Say something to her," he whispered, just loud enough for everyone to hear.

"Why don't you?" I whispered back.

"I would, but I'm not sitting next to her."

"Hey, no problem." I got out of my seat and stood up.

Suddenly the whole class was staring at me. And I realized something. Everyone was going through the first day again, but I didn't have to do the same things I did the day before.

"What is it, Jake?" Ms. Rogers asked.

"Oh, uh . . ." I felt my face start to burn with embarrassment. What was I supposed to say? "I, uh, have to go."

"The bell hasn't rung yet," Ms. Rogers replied, looking up at the clock.

Brinnggg . . . The bell rang. Everyone got up.

"What's with you?" Alex whispered in my ear, as we started toward the door.

How could I explain? I was just about to leave the room when Ms. Rogers said, "Jake?"

"Uh, yeah?" I paused.

"I'd like to have a word with you."

The other kids in the class were giving me looks and smirking. The memory of yesterday was still fresh in my mind.

Alex patted me on the shoulder. "Catch you later, Sir Jake."

Ms. Rogers waited until everyone had left the room.

"I'm sorry, Ms. Rogers," I said. "I didn't mean to interrupt."

Ms. Rogers looked puzzled. "Interrupt what?"

"Well, you know, homeroom."

"I didn't think you had," she said.

"Huh?" I didn't understand. "But that's why you asked me to stay, isn't it?"

"No." She shook her head. "I have some news I wanted to tell you."

"Oh, uh, yeah. Congratulations," I said.

"You know?" Ms. Rogers looked surprised. "How?"

"You . . . uh . . . er . . . I heard yesterday."

"But we just got back last night," she said. "It

was such a last-minute thing that we didn't have time to tell anyone."

"Oh, uh . . . that's right. I didn't hear it." I pointed at her finger. "I saw the ring."

Ms. Rogers and I both looked down at the gold band on her finger.

"Well, you're extremely observant," she said, giving me a skeptical look. "Jake, are you all right?"

"Uh, why do you ask?"

"Well, you seem a little . . . off."

I forced a smile on my face. "Must be because it's the first day of school, huh?"

Ms. Rogers smiled back. "Yes, I guess that's it. Now you better go or you'll be late for your next class."

The rest of the day went the same way. I had to be really careful not to let anyone know that I'd already been through it once. Otherwise they'd ask too many questions that I couldn't answer. Instead I did everything exactly the way I had the day before. At lunch, Alex and I talked about sitting with Amber, but used Ms. Rogers as an excuse to chicken out. I even let Alex trick me and Josh into biting into the rancid cheeseburgers. Later on I acted surprised by Mr. Dirksen's test, and watched for teachers while Alex pushed Ollie into the girls' room, knowing that Amber Sweeny would come out and tell us to grow up.

That night, Jessica made the same vegetarian spaghetti. "So how was school, Mr. Big Shot?"

"Weird," I said.

"Weird?" It was obvious that wasn't what she'd expected to hear.

"Uh-huh."

"How many sixth-graders did you wedgy?" she asked.

"None."

Once again Jessica looked surprised. "What happened to all your plans?"

I just shrugged. What good would it do to tell her how I'd gone through the first day of school two days in a row? She wouldn't believe me in a million years. And if I *really* insisted it had happened, she'd probably tell my parents and they'd probably send me to a shrink or something.

It just wasn't worth it. All I could do was pray that tomorrow would be different.

9

DAY THREE

*B*eep . . . *beep* . . . *beep!* I opened my eyes
and looked around. Was it the same, or was
it different? I jumped out of bed and went out into
the upstairs hall wearing a pair of pajama shorts.

Jessica's door was closed. I knocked.

"Jake?" she called through the door.

"Yeah, can I come in?"

"No, I'm not dressed. What is it?"

"What are you wearing?"

"What?"

"I asked what you're wearing today."

"I just told you, I'm not wearing anything yet."

"Yeah, but what will you wear when you're
wearing something?" I asked.

"Are you feeling okay?"

"Just tell me."

"Well, I guess I'll wear my black skirt and my new black top."

I started to get a sinking feeling. "The one you got at the mall last night?"

"That's right. Why?"

"Is today the first day of school?"

"Oh, come on, Jake. You know it is."

My knees felt weak. I slid down the wall and sat on the carpet in the upstairs hall, overcome by a horrible realization: *It was the first day again! I was trapped in the first day of school!* Jessica opened her door a little and peeked down at me.

"What's with you?" she asked.

"Remember how Mr. Dirksen and I switched bodies in sixth grade?" I said. "Well, it's happened again."

"You're Mr. Dirksen?" Jessica started to cover herself up.

"No, I'm Jake." Then I explained how I wasn't trapped in someone else's body this time. I was trapped in a day.

"You're trapped in the first day of school?" Jessica looked at me like I was crazy.

"You went to the pool yesterday with Cathy, right?"

"Yes."

"Well, I went to school," I said. "And the day before that, too."

Now Jessica gave me a suspicious look. "Are

you trying to say you've already done the first day of school so you don't have to go today?"

"No," I said. "I'll go. I mean, I guess I have to."

"You better. I don't think Mom and Dad would believe that you skipped school today because you'd already done it."

"But, I just want to know if you believe me," I said.

"I don't know," Jessica said. "I mean, what difference does it make? You still have to go to school today. And I'd get dressed if I were you, or you're going to be late."

I got up and went back into my room and got dressed. It might not have made a difference to my sister. But it made a big difference to me.

Later, Jessica gave me a funny look when I came into the kitchen.

"Are you okay?" she asked.

"No," I said, opening the cupboard. The unopened box of chocolate Pop-Tarts was there again, but I was getting kind of sick of them. Instead I got a bowl and filled it with granola.

"What are you doing?" Jessica asked.

"I'm having breakfast."

"You never eat granola."

"I do now," I said. "I've had chocolate Pop-Tarts for two mornings in a row and I'm getting sick of them."

"The Pop-Tarts box isn't even open, Jake."

"I know," I said. "But I opened it yesterday and the day before, too."

Jessica gave me that look again — like I'd lost my marbles. "Jake, if you opened it yesterday morning, why isn't it still open this morning?"

"Because this is yesterday all over again," I tried to explain.

My sister didn't say anything. She just stared at me.

"Okay," I said, carrying my bowl of granola over to the kitchen counter and pointing out the window. "See the bus stop?"

Jessica got up and came over. "Yes."

"In about a minute a kid with blond hair is going to show up. He'll be wearing a blue shirt, khaki pants, white tennis shoes, and carrying a green backpack. His name's Oliver but everyone calls him Ollie and he just moved here from Ohio."

The words were barely out of my mouth when Ollie arrived and looked around like he wasn't certain he was in the right place.

Jessica gave me a shocked look. "How did you know that?"

"Because he's done it for the past two days."

"Why?"

"I already told you," I said. "Because it's been the first day of school for the past two days."

My sister picked up her bowl of granola and

moved away, looking at me like I'd just escaped from the nut house.

"What are you doing?" I asked.

"I'm worried about you, Jake."

"I'm not crazy," I said. "I just told you what would happen and it happened."

Jessica nodded warily.

"I know you find it hard to believe," I said. "But this is the third first day of school in a row. Except I'm the only one who knows it."

"Is this a joke?" Jessica asked.

"I wish."

"Why are you telling me this?"

"Are you serious?" Now I looked at her like *she* she was crazy. "Wouldn't you tell people if it was happening to you?"

"I . . . I don't know," she said uncertainly.

Suddenly I realized what time it was. "The town fire siren is going to go off."

Whaaaaaa-O-Whaaaaa-O-Whaaaaa!

"How did you know that?" Jessica gasped, staring at me with wide eyes.

"I've told you five times," I said. "Better get your stuff. Cathy's sister is pulling into the driveway."

Jessica spun around and pulled back the curtain on the window that faced the driveway. Outside, a red car pulled up. She let go of the curtain and stared at me again.

"I don't understand," she said.

"Neither do I," I said.

"What are you going to do?"

"Go to school. I mean, what other choice do I have?"

The fire engines raced past as I walked down to the bus stop. Everyone was there again. Alex and I greeted each other. Then he picked on Ollie and made him run around the block.

"Like a true dweeb," Alex muttered. Then he turned to me.

"Here you go." I handed him a stick of Juicy Fruit.

Alex looked surprised. "How did you know I was going to ask for a piece of gum?"

"Teenage intuition," I said with a shrug.

10

We got to school, put our stuff in our lockers, sent Ollie on his wild-goose chase, and went in to homeroom. Then I had an idea.

"Hey, Alex, why don't you sit here?" I said, gesturing to the seat I'd sat in for the past two days.

"Why?" Alex asked.

"Why not?"

"Okay." Alex sat down and Ms. Rogers read the bulletin from Principal Blanco. Then the door opened and Amber Sweeny came in. Just as I expected, she took the seat next to Alex.

While the rest of the class stared at Amber, Alex glanced at me with wide eyes and mouthed the word, "Wow!"

"Say something to her," I whispered.

Alex glanced at Amber and shrugged. "Like what?"

"I don't know," I whispered. "You're not chicken, are you?"

"Jake?" Ms. Rogers called from the front of the room.

I quickly turned around. "Sorry."

"That's better." Ms. Rogers smiled. Then the bell rang and she asked me to stay after so she could tell me the news about her and Mr. Dirksen. I felt like I was getting into a routine.

Everything went the same until lunch, when Alex and I invoked eighth-grade privileges and cut to the front of the line. As we slid our trays along the silver rail, I remembered what we were in for.

"Cheeseburgers, boys?" asked a lunch lady wearing a hair net and plastic gloves.

"Sure," said Alex.

"No, thanks." I picked up a bag of chips and an ice cream instead.

"Health food, Sir Jake?" Alex smirked.

"Right, Sir Alex." I winked back.

We came out of the lunch line and saw Amber sitting alone.

"Check it out, Sir Jake," Alex said. "Dost thou think Princess Amber would like company?"

"Most certainly, Sir Alex," I replied, and started toward her, wondering what Alex would do.

Alex hesitated. "Art thou serious, Sir Jake?"

I stopped and looked back at him. "Why, of course, Sir Alex. Was it not your idea?"

"Well, uh . . ." Alex looked to his left. "Uh-oh."

"What is it, Sir Alex?" I asked.

"The evil witch approaches," he said, nodding at Ms. Rogers.

"So?" I asked.

"I have a bad feeling." Alex waited until Ms. Rogers stopped to chat with Amber. "Just as I thought."

I stared at Alex in amazement. "How did you know?"

"How did I know what?" Alex asked back.

"That Ms. Rogers was going to talk to Amber?"

"I didn't," Alex said. "It was just a guess."

I didn't believe him. "Listen, Alex, you can tell me. It's okay. It's not my first day of school either. I just thought I was the only one."

"What are you talking about?" Alex asked.

"I'm talking about going to school yesterday. That's how you knew Ms. Rogers was going to talk to Amber."

"You're really losing it, Jake. There was no school yesterday."

"You sure?" I squinted at him.

Alex shook his head. "Time for a serious reality check, dude. And anyway, the evil witch has foiled our plans."

I felt incredibly disappointed. For a moment I was sure Alex was going through the first day of school again just like me. But now it looked like he'd simply made a lucky guess.

Once again we arrived at the table just as Josh and Andy got there. We all sat down.

"Hey, guys, long time no see," I said in a friendly tone.

Josh and Andy gave each other surprised looks.

"So how was your summer?" I asked.

"Okay," Josh said. "Didn't see much of you."

"Yeah, I don't know what happened," I said. "Guess it went really fast."

"I guess." Josh looked a little puzzled.

Andy picked up his burger.

"I'd be careful if I were you," I said.

"Why?" Andy asked.

"I hear the burgers are a little gross."

Andy frowned and sniffed the burger. "Smells okay to me."

"They put something on it to mask the smell," I said. "I'm just warning you."

Andy took a small bite and chewed it.

"*Blech!*" He spit it out. "He's right. It's totally bogus!"

Now Josh and Alex looked down at their cheeseburgers.

"It's not just his, guys," I warned. "It's all of them."

Josh wrinkled his forehead. "How do you know, Jake?"

"Believe me," I said. "I've been there. I know."

*   *   *

After lunch we went to Mr. Dirksen's room. Once again, I made sure Alex had the seat I'd had on the two previous days. Mr. Dirksen was handing out the test when Amber Sweeny hurried in and took the seat next to Alex.

This time Alex didn't glance over at me. I guess he knew what I'd say. I nudged him anyway.

"Back off, Jake!" he hissed.

Some brave guy, huh?

"Now's your chance to say something to her," I whispered.

"I said, drop it!" Alex hissed again.

I could have kept it up, but somehow I didn't get the same charge out of goofing on Alex that he seemed to get out of goofing on me.

Meanwhile, Andy had just pointed out that Mr. Dirksen's handout looked an awful lot like a test. Just as he had on the last two days, Mr. Dirksen told us that he only wanted to see how much we knew and that we wouldn't get graded on it.

I raised my hand. "Then what's the point? You know that we don't know this stuff."

"Some of you may know some of it," Mr. Dirksen replied. "I want to use this as a baseline comparison for the tests I'll give you later in the year."

Then I got a funny idea. "What would happen if one of us aced the test?"

"I guess it would show that you knew the material," Mr. Dirksen replied.

"Wouldn't that mean that we wouldn't need to take this class this year?" I asked.

"I'll tell you what," Mr. Dirksen said with a smile. "Since I know for a fact that no one in this classroom could possibly ace this test without studying — and being this is the first day of school, none of you have studied — if it makes you happy, I'd say yes. Anyone who aces the test will not have to take my class this year."

"And we'll still get a good grade?" Josh asked.

"You'll get an *A* for the year and you won't have to show up for a single class," Mr. Dirksen said with a smug smile.

"All right!" I pumped my arm triumphantly.

"What are you so excited about?" Alex asked. "There's no way you're gonna ace it."

"Hey," I said. "You never know."

We took the test. Mr. Dirksen said he'd look them over before the end of the day and he'd let us know if anyone aced it. After class, Alex and I stopped at our lockers to dump some books. Then Amber Sweeny walked by.

"How come you didn't talk to her?" I asked Alex.

"I was gonna, but then you started talking about the test and I forgot."

That's a good one, I thought as we started down the hall.

A moment later we came face-to-face with Ollie. He stared up at us through his glasses.

"Why it's Dweeb Ollie of Ohio," Alex said. "You get to homeroom on time this morning?"

For the third day in a row Ollie told us how lost he'd gotten that morning. Then Alex dragged him toward the girls' room.

"Oh, no!" Ollie gasped and tried to squirm out of Alex's grip. Once again I was supposed to watch for teachers. Only this time, I "thought" I saw one.

"I think someone's coming," I said just before Alex could push Ollie into the girls' room. Alex let go of the sixth-grader, who quickly disappeared into the crowd.

"Where?" Alex asked, squinting down the hall. "I don't see anyone."

"Gee, you're right," I said. Then the girls' room door opened and Amber came out. She gave us a brief smile and headed down the hall.

It felt good not to be put down for once.

That day after school, I was sitting in my room, studying the parts of a cell, when Jessica knocked and came in.

"What are you doing?" she asked.

"Studying."

My sister's jaw dropped. "You? Study?"

"Sure. I've got a big science test tomorrow."

"On the *second* day of school?"

I shook my head. "Remember this morning? It'll probably be the first day all over again."

"So what am I going to do for the rest of today?" she asked.

"Well, you'll probably start your homework before dinner because you have to read a whole chapter of biology, plus geometry and world history. Then you'll make that disgusting vegetarian spaghetti for supper. Then you'll do more homework. Oh, wait. Before you do that, you'll tell me about the fire this morning. It was the home of some people who just moved in. They left the toaster oven on."

"How do you know all this?" Jessica's eyes widened and she brought her hand to her mouth.

"I keep telling you, I've done the first day of school three days in a row. I know it like the back of my hand."

"But why is it only happening to you?" she asked. "Why isn't it happening to me or anyone else?"

"Believe me," I muttered. "I wish I knew."

11

DAY FOUR

Blindfolded, I felt my way into the kitchen.

"What are you doing?" I heard Jessica ask.

"You're wearing a black top and your short black skirt," I said. "You just got the top at the mall last night. In a second you're going to ask if I'm ready for the first day of school and you're going to tell me how immature I am because I plan to wedgy sixth-graders. You're eating granola and in a little while you'll get a ride to school with Cathy and her sister."

"So?"

I pulled off the blindfold. "Aren't you curious how I knew all that stuff?"

"It's easy, Jake," she said. "You probably saw what I was wearing before you put the blindfold on. And you knew what I was going to say because that's what I always say."

"Okay," I said. "How about this? Look out the window. There's a kid at the bus stop with blond hair and glasses. His name's Oliver but everyone calls him Ollie and he's new this year."

My sister looked out the window. "So?"

"So how did I know that?" I asked.

"I don't know, Jake," Jessica said, going back to the kitchen table. "And what's the point anyway?"

Somehow it wasn't working the way I'd hoped it would. Maybe it didn't matter. It had taken a lot of energy yesterday to convince my sister that I was living through the same day over and over again, and in the long run it didn't make a difference anyway.

I went over to the kitchen cabinet, got out the peanut butter and jelly, and started to make myself a sandwich.

"That's what you're having for breakfast?" Jessica wrinkled her nose.

"This is lunch."

"But Mom left you lunch money."

"Forget it," I said. "They're serving rancid cheeseburgers at school today."

Jessica looked at me like I'd lost my mind. "How do you know *that*?"

"Believe me," I said. "By the way, in about two minutes the town fire siren's gonna go off, then Cathy's sister is gonna pull up outside. A minute or two after that some fire engines are gonna pass here on their way to a house a couple of blocks over. Some new people just moved in and they left the toaster oven on this morning and the house is gonna be pretty much destroyed."

"Did anyone ever tell you you were certifiably insane?" Jessica asked.

I knew I wasn't. But if I didn't get out of the first day of school soon, I probably would be.

Everything happened exactly as it had the morning before. In homeroom I took my old seat, the one next to the empty seat where Amber Sweeny would soon sit.

Amber came in and sat down. Everyone gave her that starstruck look and I felt Alex nudge me.

"Talk to her," he whispered.

"Okay." I turned to Amber and said, "Hi."

"Hi." Amber smiled shyly.

"You must be new this year," I said.

Amber nodded and hooked her long brown hair back behind her ear, revealing a small gold hoop earring. She had to be about the most beautiful girl who'd ever set foot in Burp It Up Middle School.

"Where're you from?" I asked.

Out of the corner of my eye, I could see Alex staring at me in absolute astonishment. But as far as I was concerned, it was a no-lose situation. Even if I made a total fool of myself, all I had to do was wait until tomorrow.

"Boulder, Colorado," Amber said.

"No kidding!" I acted really surprised. "That's about my favorite place in the whole world!"

"Really?" Amber looked surprised, too.

"Oh, man, it's got the mountains and the best skiing," I said.

"Jake, what's going on back there?" Ms. Rogers asked.

I quickly turned around and faced the front. "Uh, nothing, Ms. Rogers."

Ms. Rogers went back to reading announcements. Out of the corner of my eye I glanced at Alex and got an amazed look. Then I glanced at Amber, who gave me a smile and a shrug to let me know she was sorry I'd gotten in trouble for talking to her.

The bell rang. Amber and I both got up.

"So what's your next class?" I asked as we walked out the door.

"Uh . . ." Amber looked down at her schedule. "English. Room one-oh-two."

"It's that way," I said, pointing up the hall. "The third door on your right."

"Thanks, uh . . ."

"Jake," I said, holding out my hand. "Jake Sherman."

Amber shook it. "Thanks, Jake. I'm Amber Sweeny."

"I know."

Amber frowned. "How?"

"Ms. Rogers read your name, remember?"

"Oh, yeah." Amber grinned self-consciously. "First day in a new school, you know? It's a little confusing."

"Sure," I said. "Gets you every time."

"Well, uh . . ." Amber smiled shyly again. "See you later."

"Right." I gave her a little wave and she headed up the hall. I turned to go in the opposite direction . . . and found Alex waiting for me.

"Colorado?" He squinted at me. "Have you ever been there?"

"Well, no," I admitted.

"Then how do you know it's such a great place?"

"I saw a show on TV."

"And what is this stuff about skiing?" he asked. "You don't ski."

"Well, I plan to someday," I said.

We started walking to our next class. "I can't believe you," Alex said in awe. "I mean, you were totally cool."

"Piece of cake," I said as if it were nothing.

Alex kept shaking his head in wonder. "I just never knew you were so suave with the ladies."

The funny thing was, neither did I.

12

Everything proceeded normally until lunch. Since I'd brought mine from home, I didn't get on line with Alex. Instead I waited until Amber came out of the lunch line with her salad, then I sort of "ran into her" at the cashier.

"Hey, how's it going?" I asked, acting like I was surprised to see her.

"Pretty good," Amber said with a warm smile. "It's just hard to get used to a new school."

"I bet," I said.

"How long have you been here?" she asked.

"It's starting to seem like forever," I said, then quickly added, "but actually since sixth grade."

Amber was looking around at the tables. I could tell she wanted to sit down and eat.

"Hey, I'm sorry," I said. "You must be hungry. I shouldn't be holding you up."

"Oh, no, it's okay," Amber replied quickly. "But maybe we should sit."

Since she said "we," I figured that meant me,

too. So we found an empty table and sat down together. I asked Amber why she'd moved from Boulder, and she said her mother had gotten a job here with a printing company. Her father was a management consultant and could work just about any place he liked.

"I guess the move wasn't so hard for my parents," Amber confided. "But I just feel like I've lost all my friends."

I glanced across the cafeteria to where Josh and Andy were sitting. "I know what you mean."

Amber frowned. "But I thought you've always lived here."

"Sometimes you don't have to move to lose your friends," I said.

Just then Ms. Rogers stopped by. "Well, Jake, I see you've made friends with Amber," she said.

I sort of shrugged like it was no big deal.

"Well, I think it's nice," Ms. Rogers said. "Jake's a nice boy, Amber. I wish I could say the same for some of his friends."

Alex was coming toward us with a lunch tray. Ms. Rogers moved to the next table.

"Hi, Jake," Alex said with a funny grin. "Can I join you guys?"

"Sure," I said. He sat down and I introduced him to Amber.

"So, I see you've met Jake," Alex said.

Amber nodded and smiled.

"Yeah, old Jake." Alex gave me a playful nudge

on the shoulder. "We call him the ladies' man. Every time a new girl comes to school, he always gets to know her first."

"Really?" Amber gave me a curious look.

"No way," I said. "That's totally bogus. Nobody calls me the ladies' man."

"Oh, come on, Jake," Alex said. "Fess up."

I didn't know whether Alex made up the story to make me look bad or good. But either way, I didn't appreciate him saying that stuff in front of Amber. Not knowing what to say, I opened my lunch bag and took out my peanut butter and jelly sandwich.

"Hey, what's with the brown bag, dude?" Alex asked as he picked up his cheeseburger. "Your folks can't afford to give you lunch money?"

Alex was being completely obnoxious, probably to show off in front of Amber. I had planned to tell him the real reason I'd brought lunch from home, but now I changed my mind. Alex took a big bite of his cheeseburger and started to chew.

"We call Alex Mr. Manners," I told Amber, "because he's got such good table manners."

Suddenly Alex stopped chewing. His face turned kind of white and his eyes darted around.

"Something wrong, Mr. Manners?" I asked innocently.

"*Mmmfff.*" Alex made a funny sound. Now his face started to turn red.

"Some people talk with food in their mouths,"

I said to Amber. "But not Mr. Manners. He's much too refined."

"*Blech!*" The words were hardly out of *my* mouth when the half-chewed cheeseburger came flying out of *his*. It landed in a glob on the table. Alex quickly took a loud slurp of orange drink, rinsed out his mouth, and spit it out on the floor.

Amber's jaw fell and her green eyes widened.

"Why, Mr. Manners," I said to Alex, trying not to smile. "That's so unlike you."

Alex excused himself and disappeared for the rest of lunch. Later Amber and I walked over to Mr. Dirksen's class. Once again, Mr. Dirksen sprang the test on us, and once again I got him to agree that anyone who aced it wouldn't have to take his class for the rest of the year.

I took the test and thought I did pretty well. There were still a couple of questions I wasn't quite certain of, but I figured if I didn't ace it today, there'd always be tomorrow.

After class Alex and I stopped by our lockers to dump some books.

"So how're things with Amber?" he asked glumly.

"Okay."

"What'd she say at lunch?" he asked.

"Just how she's gonna miss the mountains and her friends and stuff."

"What else?" Alex asked.

"Not much. I said I'd show her around town after school today."

"You mean, like a date?" Alex gasped in wonder as we started down the hall.

"Well, not really."

But Alex seemed mighty impressed. "You're unreal, dude! At this rate, you'll probably get her out to the cliff by tomorrow."

The cliff was in Jeffersonville Park. It wasn't much of a cliff, really, but it had a view of Jefferson Lake, and it was the place where couples went to make out.

"No way," I said.

"But just think if you did, dude," Alex said. "You'd be a living legend at Burp It Up. The guy who got Amber Sweeny up to the cliff on the second day of school."

The idea of being a legend sort of appealed to me, although I wasn't sure getting Amber to go to the cliff was the way I wanted to do it.

"Hey, look who's coming," Alex said.

I didn't have to look. I knew it was Ollie.

Once again, Alex started to drag him toward the girls' room. As usual, I was supposed to watch for teachers.

Today I didn't see any teachers. Alex shoved Ollie into the girls' room and held the door while Ollie banged on it and shouted to let him out. The usual bunch of kids stopped to see what was going on. Then we heard Amber's voice join Ollie's, and Alex let go of the door.

That's when I just happened to step into a doorway where Amber couldn't see me. The girls' room door swung open and Ollie hurried out and started down the hall. Alex looked at the crowd around him and smiled proudly. Then Amber came out and glared at him.

"Grow up," she said, and walked away.

The crowd laughed and Alex turned a deep shade of red.

Just before the end of school I stopped at my locker to drop off some books. Alex was waiting for me, and he didn't look happy.

"Where were you?" he asked.

"When?" I played dumb.

"When Amber Sweeny came out of the girls' room and made me look like an idiot in front of half the school."

"Oh, uh, I had to go sharpen a pencil," I said.

"What?" Alex scowled at me, but before he could say anything else, Mr. Dirksen came up.

"Jake, I'm amazed," he said.

"Uh?" I pretended I didn't know what he was talking about, either.

"You almost got a perfect score," Mr. Dirksen said. "In fact, if you hadn't gotten the pseudopod mixed up with the flagellum, you would have."

"And then I could have skipped your class all year and still gotten a *A*?" I asked.

"That's right." Mr. Dirksen nodded.

"Well, maybe next time," I said.

Mr. Dirksen frowned. "But there won't be a next time."

That's what you think, I thought.

"Well, I've got to go," Mr. Dirksen said. "See you tomorrow."

He left and Alex looked at me with astonished eyes. "You are *amazing!*" he cried. "Do you realize you almost had a chance to become a legend *twice* today?"

All I could do was smile.

Just wait.

After school I showed Amber around town. Since neither of us had had much for lunch, we were hungry. We stopped at My Hero to share a cold Italian sub. She took a bite and her beautiful eyes lit up.

"This is much better than anything we have in Boulder," she said.

"There you go," I said. "Jeffersonville isn't all that bad."

"Guess not," she said with a smile.

After that we wandered into Disk Master and looked at the rows of CDs.

Suddenly Amber stopped. "Hear that?"

I paused and listened to the store music. Some

guy was singing about Norwegian Wood. "Yeah?"

"It's the Beatles," Amber said. "I used to have a baby-sitter who listened to them all the time. I think they're neat."

"My sister has some tapes of theirs," I said. At that moment I happened to glance out the window, and saw a familiar face spying on us. It was Alex. I waved at him to get lost.

"Who was that?" Amber asked. I guess she'd only caught a glimpse of him.

"Uh, no one," I said. "Guess we better get going, huh?"

"Okay."

We went outside and started to walk home. It turned out that Amber and her folks had just moved into 43 Walnut Street.

"That's only a couple of blocks away," I said. "How come I didn't see you at the bus stop this morning?"

"My dad drove me," Amber said. "We left pretty early, but of course we got totally lost. That's why I was late for homeroom."

We got to my corner and stopped.

"I could walk you home," I offered.

"No, it's all right," Amber said. "I'm pretty sure I can find my way from here."

"Well, okay." I scuffed my foot on the sidewalk, not knowing what to say next.

"It was really nice of you to show me around," Amber said, flashing her beautiful smile.

"Hey, no problem," I said.

"And thanks for everything today," she said. "I was really dreading it, you know? But you made it a lot nicer than it might have been."

"Anytime," I said.

"See ya tomorrow." Amber waved and started away. I waved back. I'd always thought beautiful girls were stuck up and snotty, but Amber was just plain nice.

Jessica was sitting in the living room when I got home.

"Where have you been?" she asked.

"I showed this new girl around town," I said.

"You sure?" she asked suspiciously.

"Yeah, why?"

"How did you know about that fire this morning?"

"I . . ." Hadn't I explained it all that morning?

"Cathy's cousin Charlie said they served bad cheeseburgers at lunch today," Jessica said. "How did you know about that?"

Now that I thought of it, maybe I hadn't explained it this morning. I stepped into the living room, planning to sit down and explain everything. But Jessica quickly jumped up and stood behind the chair.

"Not too close, Jake," she warned.

"What?"

"I don't know what's going on, but I don't like it," Jessica said.

"And I don't know what you're talking about."

"I'm talking about what you did today," Jessica said accusingly. "I heard you planning things with that jerk Alex on the phone last night. I now you planned to wedgy all the sixth-graders. The part I didn't hear was that you were going to burn down a house and try to poison the whole school."

"You've gone psycho," I said.

"Then how could you know about those things before they happened?" Jessica asked.

"Because this is the fourth day in a row that I've gone to the first day of school," I tried to explain. "I know everything that's going to happen."

Jessica backed away from the chair toward the stairs. "You expect me to believe that?"

"You have to believe it," I said. "It's true."

Jessica reached the banister. "Of course, Jake. I believe you." The next thing I knew, she ran up the stairs.

"Hey! Where are you going!" I yelled.

"Don't try to stop me!" Jessica yelled back.

I ran to the bottom of the stairs. *Bang!* A door slammed upstairs.

"What are you doing?" I shouted. I ran up the stairs and tried her door, but it was locked.

"It's for your own good!" Jessica shouted from inside.

"What are you talking about?" I yelled.

Inside, I could hear Jessica on the phone. "Hello, Mom? I think you better come home right away. No, no, everybody's okay, but we have a problem with Jake. A *big* problem."

Of course, the joke was on Jessica, even though it wasn't one I wanted to play. She got both of my parents to come home from work early, but when they called the fire department, the fire chief insisted that the blaze wasn't arson. They had traced it to the toaster oven. The same thing happened when my father called the board of education. The district nutritionist said the meat problem had been caused by a faulty refrigeration unit in the Burp-It-Up kitchen.

My parents were really mad at Jessica, but I finally got some time to brush up on my pseudopods and flagellums. I couldn't wait until the next day.

13

DAY FIVE

The next morning I was in a really great mood.

"What's with you?" Jessica asked, watching me from the kitchen table where she was eating her granola.

"Huh?" I looked up from the toast I was buttering.

"You're whistling."

"Oh, uh, yeah." I couldn't help smiling.

"You didn't forget that it's the first day of school, did you?"

"Nope." I munched on a piece of toast.

"Of course not, Mr. Big Shot. This is the day you and Alex conquer the world, right?"

I wasn't going to argue with her. Instead, I said, "Hey, do you still have that old Beatles tape?"

"Uh, I think so."

"Think I could borrow it?" I opened a cabinet

and took out the small plastic cooler my parents used on trips.

"I guess so." Jessica scowled. "What are you doing with the cooler?"

"Just taking it to school." I opened the refrigerator and took out the freeze packs we used to keep things cold.

"Aren't you going to put anything else in there?" Jessica asked after I put the freeze packs in the cooler.

"Not yet," I said. "By the way, you think I could catch a ride with you to school this morning?"

"How did you know I was getting a ride?" Jessica asked.

"Just a guess."

"Well, I guess it'll be okay."

"And do you think we could stop at My Hero on the way?" I asked.

"Why?" Jessica looked at me like I'd flipped.

"I just want to pick up something for lunch," I said.

I got Cathy's sister to stop at the sub shop just long enough for me to run inside and buy a cold Italian hero. At school I met Alex at our lockers.

"Hey, I thought we were gonna meet at the bus stop this morning," he said, holding the letter with his combination.

"Something came up," I said. "So how'd it go?"

Before he could answer, Ollie ran up to us red-faced and out of breath, so I knew Alex had made him run around the block.

"Why, if it isn't Ollie from Ohio," Alex said, then turned to me. "Ollie's a new sixth-grader and it looks like he missed the bus."

"You made me miss it," Ollie gasped.

"Now, now, Ollie, you just have to learn to run faster," Alex said.

"Anyway, now I'm late and I can't find my homeroom," he said.

"And what room might that be, Ollie boy?" Alex asked.

"One-oh-six."

Alex gave him that awestruck look. "Oh, wow, that's all the way around to the other side of school!" he gasped, giving me a wink.

"Don't listen to this goofball," I said. "It's just two doors down on your left."

"Okay, thanks." Ollie quickly jogged away.

"What'd you do that for?" Alex asked.

"You already made him run all the way to school," I said. "Don't you think that's enough?"

Alex shrugged and we went into homeroom. Amber showed up late as usual and Alex dared me to talk to her. Once again I did. Later in the hall Alex grilled me about Colorado and skiing.

"Dude, I can't believe you," he said in awe. "I mean, you were totally cool."

"Piece of cake," I said like it was nothing.

Alex kept shaking his head in wonder. "I never knew you were so suave with the ladies."

"Oh, yeah, always," I said with a smile. "Matter of fact, I bet I can get her to the cliff by this afternoon."

Alex laughed. "No way!"

"Bet?" I said.

"You'll lose big time."

"Put your money where your mouth is, dude."

"Okay, ten bucks says you can't do it," Alex said.

"Deal." We shook hands.

I didn't see Amber until lunch, when I once again "bumped" into her outside the cashier. We talked a little and then decided to sit down. Only this time, instead of bringing a peanut butter and jelly sandwich from home, I took the cold Italian hero out of the cooler.

"My favorite!" she gasped.

"Here, have half," I said, offering part to her.

"I couldn't," Amber said. "It's your lunch."

"It's cool, really," I said. "I can't eat the whole thing."

Amber accepted half of the sandwich, and we talked and laughed all through lunch. Ms. Rogers came by and said hi, but Alex stayed away because that was part of our deal.

After lunch, Amber and I walked to Mr. Dirksen's room and sat down together. A moment later Andy and Josh came in.

"Be right back," I told Amber.

I got up and went over to my old friends. I'd only planned to say hello, since I hadn't had a chance to talk to them at lunch.

"Look who's here," Josh said.

"Hey, guys, didn't see much of you this summer," I said, trying to be friendly.

"We were around," Andy said. "Where were you?"

"He was around," Josh answered before I could. "He just had cooler friends to hang out with."

"That's not exactly true," I said in a low voice so Alex wouldn't hear.

"Oh, yeah?" Josh asked. "Then how come we didn't see you all summer?"

"I don't know," I said defensively. "I guess it just went by really fast."

"We hear you're a really fast kind of guy these days," Andy said sarcastically. "Alex is telling everyone you bet him ten bucks you could get that new girl Amber Sweeny over to the cliff this afternoon."

That made me mad. Alex wasn't supposed to tell anyone.

"So cool," Josh muttered.

"It's a joke," I whispered. "I can't lose."

81

"Jake really thinks he's hot stuff," Andy said.

"Yeah," Josh said bitterly. "No wonder he doesn't want to hang out with dorks like us."

It wasn't fair. Here I was, trying to be friendly, and they wouldn't give me a chance. Then I got an idea.

"Hey," I said in a low voice. "I hear Dirksen's gonna give us a surprise test today."

"On the first day of school?" Andy shook his head. "No way."

"It's not gonna count," I said. "He just wants to see what we know."

It didn't take long to make another bet, this one for ten bucks each that I could ace the test. Of course, they had to promise to pay me by dinnertime.

A few minutes later I took the test for the fifth time. After class, Alex and I stopped by our lockers to dump our books.

"So how's it going, lover boy?" Alex asked.

"You weren't supposed to tell anyone about the bet," I said. "What if someone tells Amber?"

"Hey, don't worry," Alex said. "Everyone's cool."

We started down the hall and ran into Ollie. Once again, Alex shoved him into the girls' room and held the door while Ollie banged on it and shouted to let him out. The usual crowd of kids stopped to see what was going on.

"Let him out," I said.

"What?" Alex looked surprised.

"I said, let him out."

"Why?" Alex asked.

"Yeah, Jake," said a kid in the crowd. "It's funny."

"How would you like to be trapped in the girls' room?" I asked.

"Chill out, Jake," Alex said.

"You let him out or else," I said, making a fist. "I mean it, Alex."

Alex let go of the door and Ollie raced out and down the hall. Then Amber came out and fixed a steely gaze on Alex, who shrank back into the crowd.

"Grow up," she said with a glower. Then she turned to me and smiled. "I heard what you said."

"It's just not right to pick on little kids," I said. "Especially when they're new in town."

As we started to walk to our next class, I glanced back over my shoulder at Alex. He was staring at me with a totally dumbfounded look on his face.

Just before the end of school, I stopped at my locker to drop off some books. I knew Alex would be waiting for me, but I didn't expect to find Josh and Andy, too. And they didn't look happy.

"Hey, guys," I said a little warily.

"Nice going, Jake," Josh muttered.

"How'd you ace that test?" Andy asked.

I shrugged. "Luck, I guess."

"Bull," Josh said, reaching into his pocket and handing me ten dollars.

"Yeah, I don't know how you did it, Jake," Andy said, giving me his ten dollars, "but you really conned us."

"Way to go, *friend*," Josh said sourly. Then he turned to Andy. "Come on, let's get out of here before Jake figures out another way to rob us."

Josh and Andy left. I watched them walk away down the hall. Suddenly I felt really bad.

"Why the long face, dude?" Alex asked, coming up.

I wasn't about to tell him. Actually, I was surprised he was talking to me. "How come you're not mad that I made you let Ollie out of the girls' room?" I asked.

"I don't know," Alex said. "Maybe it was dumb to push him in there in the first place."

I nodded, still watching Josh and Andy walk away.

"Aw, don't worry about those chumps," Alex said. "They're just a couple of losers. I know why you made that bet with them."

"You do?" I asked, surprised.

"Sure," Alex said with a grin. "You just wanted to make sure you were covered when you lost your bet with me."

"Yeah, right," I said, feeling glum and wishing I had my old friends back.

After school I showed Amber around town just as I had the day before. Only this time I brought along a little boom box and played Jessica's old Beatles tape.

"You like them?" Amber stopped on the sidewalk and stared at me with raised eyebrows.

"Oh, yeah, they're one of my favorite groups."

"Mine, too!" Amber gasped.

For a second, Amber and I just looked into each other's eyes.

"It's so strange," she said. "But I feel like I've met you before."

Suddenly I had to look away.

"Uh, know what?" I said. "There's one other place I want to show you — Jeffersonville Park."

It wasn't hard to get Amber into the park, and once we were there I told her I wanted to show her the cliff because it had a good view. We were walking up the path when I saw Alex and a bunch of guys from school coming toward us.

"Hey, dude!" Alex grinned and winked. "Headin' for the cliff, huh?" All the kids with him smiled knowingly.

"Yeah," I said. "I'm just showing Amber around."

"Well, have a good time, dude," Alex said, and winked again.

Alex and his buddies continued down the path, and Amber and I headed for the cliff.

"What was that about?" Amber asked.

"Huh?" I played dumb.

"It seemed like they were waiting for you."

"Naw, a lot of people hang out in this park after school," I lied.

I took Amber up to the cliff and showed her the view. Then we walked home and stopped at my corner again. I pretended to be surprised that we both lived in the same neighborhood.

"I could walk you home," I said, knowing she'd say no.

"No, it's all right," Amber said. "I'm pretty sure I can find my way from here."

"Well, okay." I scuffed my foot on the sidewalk.

"It was really nice of you to show me around," Amber said, flashing her beautiful smile.

"No problem."

"And thanks for everything today," she said. "I was really dreading it, you know? But you made it a lot better than it could have been."

"Hey, anytime," I said, trying to smile.

"See ya tomorrow." Amber waved and started away. I waved back. For the second time that day I felt lousy about winning a bet. I'd used my friends, and then I'd used Amber.

Alex was waiting at my house. With a big smile he reached into his pocket and dug out a crumpled ten-dollar bill.

"Here you go, dude!" he said, giving it to me.

"I never saw anyone so happy about losing a bet," I said, putting the money in my wallet.

"Are you kidding?" Alex slapped me on the back. "It was worth it! Tomorrow everyone will know that my best bud is the dude who got Amber Sweeny up to the cliff on the first day of school! You're a legend, dude!"

I tried to smile, but somehow I didn't feel like a legend.

That night Jessica cooked vegetarian spaghetti again. Just the smell of it made me want to barf.

"So how was school, Mr. Big Shot?" she asked.

"Okay," I said. "Have you ever heard of someone having to go through the same day over and over?"

She gave me a strange look. "No, why?"

"Just wondering."

"So, did you wedgy everyone in sight?"

I shook my head. It was hard to believe that five days ago I thought that was the coolest thing in the world.

"What happened to all your plans with Alex?" she asked.

"I don't know."

"Is something wrong?" Jessica asked.

"You think tomorrow night we could have something other than spaghetti?"

"Of course. I never make the same dinner twice."

That's what you think, I thought.

Jessica gave me a funny look. "What's with you?"

"Nothing."

"Remember that fire this morning?" she asked.

"Yeah . . . er . . . I mean no . . . er, I mean yeah?" It was getting hard to keep track of what I was supposed to know and not know.

"It was just a few blocks over," she said. "A new family just moved in. I heard they left the toaster oven on. There's hardly anything left."

"That's really too bad," I said.

I spent the rest of the night watching TV. We had cable and got about sixteen channels so I figured I had sixteen days before I'd have to start renting videos. But it wasn't a very reassuring thought. How long could I go through the first day of school before I went crazy?

14

DAY SIX

Beep . . . beep . . . beep! The alarm went off but I didn't get out of bed. What was the point? I knew exactly what was going to happen. Why should I listen to Jessica give me a hard time again? Why bother hanging around with Alex and getting hassled by Josh and Andy? About the only thing I could look forward to was seeing Amber, but I really didn't want to play any more tricks on her. In fact, I wished I could go over to her house and just tell her the truth about the day before.

But it was a new first day of school and right now she didn't even know who I was.

Still, I wished I could go over to Walnut Street and see her.

Walnut Street . . .

WALNUT STREET!!!

I sat straight up in bed. The fire in the toaster oven. . . . The house was a couple of blocks over. . . . A new family . . .

Why hadn't I put it together sooner?

I jumped out of bed and quickly pulled on my clothes. They were the same clothes I'd worn the day before, but today they were clean again, so it didn't matter. Still tucking my shirt in, I stumbled out into the hall. Jessica, wearing an oversized T-shirt, was just coming out of her room.

"What are you doing?" she asked with a yawn.

"I've got to go somewhere."

"Now? What about the first day of school?"

"Don't worry."

"You're not going to skip it, are you?" she asked.

"Believe me, it doesn't matter."

I ran down the stairs and out the door. Walnut was three streets over. I had to hurry. Amber had said she and her father left early.

I ran down Bay Drive, past Cedar and Oak to Walnut. As I turned the corner, I saw a yellow car backing out of a driveway about halfway down the block. I started to run even faster. Luckily, the car turned toward me. It had green license plates. As I got closer I saw that they said COLORADO in white letters. I ran into the middle of the street, waving my arms for the car to stop.

The car stopped and Amber's father rolled down

his window. Like Amber, he had brown hair.

"Can I help you?" He looked puzzled. I could see Amber looking across the front seat at me.

"Listen," I said, gasping for breath. "You have to go back to your house. You left your toaster oven on."

"What? That can't be."

"Look, Mr. Sweeny," I gasped. "You have to believe me. Your house is gonna burn down."

Mr. Sweeny frowned. "Who are you? How do you know my name?"

"I don't have time to explain," I said. "Now, do you want to save your house or not?"

Mr. Sweeny looked across the seat at Amber and then back at me. "I'm sorry, son, but it's just not possible."

"It is," I insisted. "You have to believe me."

"But we don't own a toaster oven."

Huh? For a second I didn't understand. Then I thought maybe I did.

"Sure you do," I said. "Look, I can't argue with you now. Maybe they call it something else in Colorado, but if you don't get back in your house and turn it off, you're gonna have a fire."

Mr. Sweeny looked at Amber again and then back at me. "I think you have the wrong people, son." He started to close his window.

"Wait!" I shouted, putting my hand on the window. "You have to believe me. There's gonna be a fire. Your house is gonna burn down."

91

Whaaaaa-O-Whaaaaa-O-Whaaaa! The town's fire siren began to blast.

"You see?" I said.

Mr. Sweeny and Amber turned to look back at the house. Nothing unusual was happening. There was no smoke, no fire. . . . Mr. Sweeny looked at me.

"How did you know there was going to be a fire?" he asked.

"I don't get it," I said.

"Maybe it's just a coincidence, right, son?" Mr. Sweeny said.

Eeeeiiiiirrrrnnnn! Eeeeiiiiirrrrnnnn! Now we could hear the sounds of the fire trucks in the distance. The sirens gradually grew louder as the trucks came nearer. Once again we all looked back at the Sweenys' house. There was still nothing unusual.

Then I noticed a plume of black smoke rising in the air. It was coming from one street over: Maple!

"It's not your house!" I gasped.

A second later the big red-and-silver pumper truck raced past on Bay Drive with its lights flashing, followed by the second truck. I started running toward Maple Street. When I got there, the firemen were already pulling hoses off the pumper and hooking them up to the fire hydrant. The second house in from the corner was burning. Flames leaped out of some of the windows, along with thick black smoke.

A crowd of neighbors was forming on the sidewalk to watch as the firemen began to spray powerful streams of water into the windows and on the roof.

"Who lives there?" I heard a woman with her hair in rollers ask.

"I don't know," said another woman wearing a pink robe and fuzzy slippers. "I think they just moved in yesterday."

"Was anyone home?"

"I don't think so."

"Oh, those poor people."

I watched them fight the fire. Imagine living in a house for just one day and then coming home and finding it destroyed.

Then I realized I had to get to school. Of course, I didn't really have to go through the first day again, but if I didn't, it would be super hard to explain to my parents and the school why not.

I got down to the bus stop just in time to see Alex order everyone to stand in a row. When he saw me, he raised his hand high. "Sir Jake, dude!"

"Hi, Alex." I gave him a high five.

"Are we the Knights of Wedgy?" Alex asked loudly enough for everyone to hear.

"Uh, listen, can I talk to you for a second?" I said, motioning him away from the group.

"Sure, what's up?" Alex asked.

"I know last night I agreed to be a Knight of Wedgy," I said in a low voice. "But I changed my mind. Let's just go to school, okay? No wedgies."

Alex stared at me. "Chicken?"

I stared back at him. Now I understood why Amber told him to grow up. "Yeah." I nodded. "I'm a big fat chicken."

"Then I'll do it myself," Alex said, turning back to the group. The only kid who wasn't in line was Ollie.

Alex peered down at him and rubbed his chin. "Hmmm. What manner of creature is this? Must be a dweeb. Tell me, dweeb, do you have trouble hearing?"

Ollie shook his head.

"Leave him alone," I said.

Alex turned and frowned at me. "What's with you?"

"I told you, I don't want to pick on anyone."

Alex stared past me across the street, where old Mr. MacDowell was just coming out of his house.

"Okay, then watch this," he said, going across the street, and moving the garbage can into the driveway. But before Mr. MacDowell could hit it, I went over and moved it out of the way.

"What'd you do that for?" Alex asked when I came back to the bus stop.

94

"Just give it a rest," I said.

The bus came and we all got on. Alex went to the back. "Okay, everyone, move out. Eighth-graders only."

The other kids moved and Alex waved to me. "Come on, dude. We've got the back of the bus. Eighth-grade privileges."

Ollie had taken a seat near the front. He was looking up at me.

"I'm gonna sit here," I told Alex and sat down next to the sixth-grader. "Hi, bet your name's Ollie."

He gave me an astonished look. "How'd you know?"

All I could do was smile. "It's a long story."

We got to school and I helped Ollie with his locker combination and showed him where his homeroom was. When I got to my homeroom, Alex waved to me from the back, but I took a seat across the room instead. When Amber came in I hid my face in a book so she wouldn't notice me.

At lunch I sat with Andy and Josh and warned them about the cheeseburgers. Then I told them about the surprise science test and what the answers would be. I'd taken the test so many times that I knew it by heart. Josh and Andy both made up little crib sheets.

In Mr. Dirksen's class I took a seat in the front

with Andy and Josh, and hid my face again so Amber wouldn't see me when she came in. I got Mr. Dirksen to agree let anyone who aced the test skip this class for the rest of the year. Andy and Josh used their crib sheets. After class we met in the hall.

"How'd you guys do?" I asked.

"I'm sure I aced it!" Josh said. "You gave us every single answer!"

"Yeah." Andy grinned. "I wish we could be there when Dirksen marks it. He's gonna freak!"

"Guess we're all gonna have a free period after lunch for the rest of the year!" Josh slapped me on the back. "Way to go, Jake!"

The three of us gave each other high fives and laughed. It was just like old times.

Suddenly we noticed a commotion down the hall. Alex was pushing Ollie into the girls' room and the usual crowd was gathering around them.

"Silver's such a jerk," Andy muttered.

"Hey, cool it," cautioned Josh. "He's Jake's good buddy now."

"Forget it," I said, "the guy's a bozo."

Once again I went down the hall and told Alex to let Ollie out of the girls' room or else. Alex let go of the door and Ollie hurried out, followed by Amber. Our eyes locked for a second, but before she could say anything I turned and took off.

*   *   *

At the end of the day I went to my locker to put away some books before I caught the bus home.

"Jake?"

I turned around and found Mr. Dirksen with Josh and Andy. Mr. Dirksen looked serious. Josh and Andy had sheepish looks on their faces.

"I find it very interesting that you three close friends somehow managed to get perfect scores on the test this afternoon," he said. "Could you please explain that to me?"

"Sure," I said with a grin. "We're all brilliant."

Mr. Dirksen wasn't amused. "I don't know how you found out about it, but I'm certain you did. And now I assume that all three of you expect to skip my class the rest of the year."

"Well, that's the deal we made," I said.

"You're right," Mr. Dirksen said. "And a deal's a deal. So all I'll need is a letter from each of your parents stating that they agree that you don't have to take science this year."

"But that's not fair," Josh complained.

"I'm sorry, Josh, but I can't excuse students from my class for the entire year without their parents' consent," Mr. Dirksen said. "And don't bother forging the letters because I'll be calling each of your homes to confirm."

Mr. Dirksen left. Josh, Andy, and I looked at each other and shrugged.

"Come on," Josh said. "We better get out to

the parking lot or we'll miss our buses."

We started walking.

"You gonna ask your parents for a letter?" Andy asked.

Josh shook his head. "Get real. They'll never let me skip class for the whole year."

"Neither will mine," I said.

Andy nodded. "Mine, neither. Well, I just wish we could've been there when Dirksen graded those things. I bet he really wigged."

We all smiled at the thought.

"You guys didn't tell him I gave you the answers, did you?" I asked.

"No way!" Josh looked offended. "What do you think we are?"

I smiled. Josh and Andy would never squeal. On the other hand, I had a feeling Alex probably would have spilled his guts in no time.

"So you doin' anything after school?" Andy asked me.

"Naw, what about you?"

"Want to play some ball?"

"Sure."

"Great," Josh said. "We'll meet at my house."

We got out to the parking lot and split up to catch our buses. It was good to have my old friends back.

The first person I saw on the bus home was Ollie, so I sat down next to him.

"How're you doin'?" I asked as the bus pulled away from school.

"Okay," he said. "Thanks for getting me out of the girls' room before."

"No sweat. How was the first day of school?"

"Okay, I guess," Ollie said.

"You're new in town, right?"

"I'll say. We just moved in yesterday."

"Yesterday?" For some reason that sounded vaguely familiar.

"Yeah," Ollie said. "It was a real last-minute thing. My father got a transfer and we had to move really quick so that I could start the year in a new school."

Something about this was beginning to bother me. "How come you got to the bus stop so early this morning?" I asked.

"Well, my parents had to go away for the day and I didn't want to stay home alone so I figured I'd wait at the bus stop," he said.

It was starting to bother me more. "What street do you live on?"

"Maple Street," Ollie said as the bus bumped and squeaked along. Why?"

"Which house?"

"Second one from the corner." Ollie gave me a puzzled look. I felt dizzy, like all the blood had drained out of my face.

"What'd you have for breakfast this morning?" I asked, praying I was mistaken.

"Some waffles."

Suddenly I felt relieved. "Made them in a waffle iron?"

"No, they were frozen," Ollie said. "I made them in the toaster oven."

15

We got off at the bus stop. I knew I couldn't let Ollie walk home alone and find that his home had burned down, so I pretended my house was near his.

"So, uh, will your parents be home when you get there?" I asked.

Ollie gave me another funny look and then shook his head. "They said they wouldn't be home until late. Why?"

"Just asking. Tell you what? Want to hang out at my house until they come home?"

Ollie frowned. "Thanks, but I better get home. They might try to call."

A sense of dread was growing inside me with every step. Ollie was just about to have the worst shock of his life, and there was nothing I could do to stop it.

As we turned the corner and started walking up Maple Street, a faint smell of smoke was in the air. I glanced at Ollie, but he didn't seem to notice it. Then Ollie's house came into view. Maybe I should say, what was left of Ollie's house. The walls and part of the roof were still standing, but the house was charred and gutted. Every window was broken and the lawn was covered with smoldering chairs and couches the firefighters had pulled out from inside.

Ollie stopped and blinked. Then he started to run toward the house.

"Ollie!" I started to run after him. "Ollie, don't go inside!"

He stopped halfway up the driveway and just looked around. Tears ran down his cheeks, and he took off his glasses and wiped his eyes with his hand. For a long time he didn't say anything. Then he turned and looked up at me.

"You knew about this," he said. "That's why you were so friendly to me. That's why you walked with me."

I shook my head. "I knew this house had burned, but I didn't know it was yours until we were on the bus just now."

"How'd it happen?"

"I heard it was . . ." I stopped myself.

"What?" Ollie asked.

"Nothing," I said. There was no point in telling him he'd left the toaster oven on. It would only make him feel worse. "Is there any way you can get in touch with your parents?"

Ollie shook his head. "They had to go to the city

on business. They told me to come home after school and wait for them."

We left a note saying that he'd be at my house. We walked over there and sat in the kitchen eating potato chips and drinking Cokes.

Then Jessica came home and I told her what had happened.

"That's terrible," Miss Politically Correct said. "What time do you think your parents will get home?"

"I don't know," he said. "They warned me it might be kind of late."

"Maybe you ought to stay for dinner," she said. "I'm making spaghetti."

"Couldn't you make something else?" I asked.

Jessica frowned. "What's wrong with my spaghetti?"

"I . . . er . . . Ollie may not be used to vegetarian spaghetti."

"It's okay," Ollie said. "I don't have much of an appetite anyway."

I sighed. It looked like I was going to be eating that disgusting spaghetti for the sixth night in a row.

We sat around and Ollie talked about moving here from Ohio, and how everything was so new. New house (until this morning), new neighborhood, new school, new grade.

"In fifth grade you're one of the big kids," he

said. "Then you get to middle school and suddenly you're a little kid all over again. And all these big kids want to push you around."

"The eighth-graders are the worst," Jessica said, shooting me a look from the kitchen counter.

"I'll say." Ollie nodded in agreement.

I shrank down in my seat and didn't say a word.

"I bet you'll want to push the sixth-graders around when you're in eighth grade," Jessica said, making sure I heard.

"I hope not," Ollie said.

"I think that's very mature of you," Jessica said, giving me another pointed look.

If I'd slouched down any farther in my chair I probably would have wound up on the floor.

We were in the middle of dinner when the doorbell rang. Ollie instantly looked up.

"I bet that's your folks," I said, getting up. "Better get your stuff."

I went to the front door and opened it. A short, grim-looking man wearing a suit and glasses was standing there. He had the same sandy-colored hair as Ollie. Standing behind him was a woman trying to rub tears out of her eyes.

"Are you Jake Sherman?" the man asked.

"Yes. Ollie's just getting his stuff," I said. "I'm really sorry about your house."

Ollie's father nodded and his mother sniffled. Ollie came up behind me and went through the doorway.

"Thank God, you're all right!" His mom cried and hugged him.

Ollie's father held out his hand. "Thank you, Jake. Thank you very much."

I watched as Ollie's parents led him back to their car. They'd come all the way from Ohio and now they had no place to live. They'd probably lost all their possessions, too.

Just before they got in the car, Ollie turned and waved. "See you tomorrow."

I waved back, and watched as they drove away. Suddenly it occurred to me that I should have invited them to stay at our house for the night. But by then it was too late. The car turned the corner and disappeared. I didn't know where they were going. I went back to the kitchen where Jessica was waiting for me.

"Were you one of the eighth-graders who picked on him?" she asked.

"No."

"What happened to all your plans with Alex? I thought you two were supposed to be the Knights of Wedgy today."

"I guess I changed my mind," I said with a shrug.

"Wow," Jessica said. "That means there still might be hope for you."

I tried to smile, but it wasn't easy. The truth was, things looked pretty hopeless.

16

DAY SEVEN

Beep . . . *beep* . . . *beep!* As soon as the alarm went off I jumped out of bed and got dressed. As I stepped out into the upstairs hall, Jessica opened her door. She rubbed her eyes and yawned.

"Where are you going?"

"I have to take care of something," I said.

"What about breakfast?"

"I'll get something at school." I dashed downstairs and out of the house. The dew was still on the grass, and grown-ups wearing suits were walking out of their houses and heading for the train station.

I ran down Bay Drive and turned onto Maple. A moment later I jogged up Ollie's driveway, and rang the doorbell.

"Uh, who is it?" Ollie asked from inside.

"Jake Sherman," I said. "I'm an eighth-grader and I've been assigned to help you through the first day of school because you're new here. I'm supposed to make sure you find the bus stop and get your locker open and find your homeroom."

But Ollie didn't open the door. "Nobody told us about that."

"That's probably because you just moved in yesterday," I ad-libbed.

"Well, okay," Ollie said. "But would you mind waiting outside? I'm here alone and my parents told me not to let anyone in."

"Uh, normally I would, Ollie, but I really need to use the bathroom."

"How'd you know to call me Ollie?" he asked through the door.

"Uh, I didn't," I quickly said. "It was just an accident. I, er, had a friend named Oliver once and we called him Ollie, too."

"Well, I'm sorry, but you'll have to wait," Ollie said. "I really promised my parents I wouldn't let anyone in."

I had no choice but to wait. After a while, Ollie came out and gave me a funny look. "You *sure* you're from school?"

"Positive," I said. "And the first thing I'm supposed to do is make sure you've turned off all your appliances."

"Huh?" Ollie looked at me very strangely.

"The school doesn't want any homes burning down."

"I'm sure it's okay," Ollie said.

"I'm sure, too," I said. "But you don't want me to get in trouble with the school, do you?"

"Well, okay, wait a second." Ollie went back inside. A moment later he came back out. "Okay, let's go."

"Uh, you *sure* you checked *all* your appliances?" I asked. It seemed like he'd been in and out awful fast.

"Yeah." Ollie started down the driveway, then stopped and looked back at me. "Now what?"

"Well, er, uh . . ." I had to think fast. "There was just a story on the news last night about faulty toaster ovens. You wouldn't happen to have a toaster oven, would you?"

Ollie nodded.

"Wow," I said. "Would you do me a super-huge favor and check it again? Just to make sure."

"Are you for real?" Ollie looked at me like I was a total dork.

"That's all I ask," I said. "Okay?"

Ollie rolled his eyes and went back into the house again. This time he stayed inside a little longer, and when he came out, he looked at me suspiciously.

"That was weird," he said. "The toaster oven

was still on. And it was really hot. I bet it could have started a fire."

Whew! A huge feeling of relief spread through me. That was close.

The rest of the day went pretty well. I protected Ollie from Alex, and sat next to Amber again. I talked to her, but this time I didn't make any bets with anyone. And while I was friendly to Andy and Josh, I didn't give them advance warning about Mr. Dirksen's test. I did warn them about the cheeseburgers, and at lunch the three of us sat with Amber.

It was tough not to put down all the right answers on the test, but I figured I'd save them for when it really counted. After school I showed Amber around town for a while and then went over to Josh's to play ball. I even invited Alex so that we could play two-on-two. He turned out to be a decent basketball player, and we all had a good time.

"So how was school, Mr. Big Shot?" Jessica asked that night in the kitchen as she started to boil the water for spaghetti.

"Hey," I said. "What do you say we order in a pizza?"

Jessica frowned. "Mom didn't leave us money."

"I'll pay," I said. I was so sick of her vegetarian spaghetti I would have paid *double* for a pizza.

"Did I hear you right?" Jessica asked. *"You're* going to pay for a pizza for *both* of us?"

"I'll even order half vegetarian," I said, knowing that was her favorite politically correct pizza.

Jessica stared at me suspiciously. "Is there something you're not telling me? Did you break something of mine? Or is there some huge favor you're going to ask?"

"No." I smiled. "I just want you to know how much I appreciate having a big sister."

Jessica got the portable phone and handed it to me. "Here. Order it fast before you change your mind."

17

DAY EIGHT

Beep . . . beep . . . beep! I opened my eyes. I couldn't believe I was going to do it all over again but what choice did I have? I jumped out of bed, pulled on my clothes, and headed out. As I stepped into the upstairs hall, Jessica opened her door. This time she just rubbed her eyes, yawned, and shook her head.

Outside, the dew was on the grass again and the grown-ups were heading for work. I arrived at Ollie's house about the same time I had the day before and rang the bell.

A moment later the door opened and I found myself facing Ollie's mom.

"Yes?" she looked a little puzzled.

"Uh, you're not supposed to be here," I said.

Ollie's mom scowled, then smiled as if she

understood. "We just moved in. You must be looking for the Kreegers, the people who used to live here."

"No, I'm looking for Ollie," I said.

Just then Ollie came up behind his mom. "Oh, hi, Jake, don't tell me you've been assigned to help me again."

Again?

Now his mom smiled. "You must be the nice boy Ollie told us about last night."

Last night? "Uh, I didn't know Ollie last night," I said.

Ollie and his mom gave each other strange looks. Then Ollie said, "Come on, Jake. Stop kidding. You came here yesterday to make sure I got to school okay. The toaster oven, remember?"

"You mean, today's not yesterday?" I asked.

Both Ollie and his mother frowned.

"What I meant was, today's not the first day of school?" I said.

"Of course not," Ollie's mom said. "Yesterday was the first day of school."

"I don't believe it!" I cried. "It's the second day of school!"

Ollie and his mom looked at me like I was nuts.

"I don't think we'll need your help today," his mom said, putting her arm protectively around Ollie's shoulder. "I think he'll be able to find the way himself."

"See you at school, Jake." Ollie waved, and his mother closed the door.

I staggered back down the driveway. *It was the second day of school!* I couldn't believe it! Out in the street I started to run home. As I crossed Walnut, a horn beeped and a yellow car with green Colorado license plates stopped in front of me. Amber rolled down her window.

"Need a ride to school, Jake?" she asked.

"Uh . . . uh, sure!"

Then Amber looked at my clothes and frowned. "Didn't you go home last night?"

"Well, yeah," I said. "What makes you think —" Suddenly I stopped and looked down at my clothes . . . *They were the same clothes I'd worn yesterday!*

"On second thought, thanks for the offer," I said. "But I think I'll just go home first and change."

"Okay, see you at school," Amber said.

When I got home, Jessica was sitting at the kitchen table, eating granola.

"How come you went out early again this morning?" she asked.

"Uh, I just had to," I said, heading for the stairs.

"And you won't tell me why, right?" she said.

"You wouldn't believe it anyway," I said as I started up the stairs.

"How many more mornings is this going to go on?" she called.

Halfway up the stairs I stopped. "You know what?" I yelled back happily. "I think it's finally over!"

HELP!

I'm Trapped
in the First Day
of Summer Camp

To Geoff, bon voyage!

1

"Just be yourself," said my sister, Jessica. "Just try your best," said my father.

"Just remember to brush your teeth," said my mother.

We were sitting in the kitchen, having breakfast. They were giving me advice before I went away to camp for the first time.

"Thanks, guys, I'll remember all that." I yawned and stretched my arms.

Mom narrowed her eyes and studied me closely. "You look tired. Didn't you sleep last night?"

"Sure, I did," I said, even though I'd hardly slept at all.

"No way," said Jessica. "He was up all night tossing and turning in bed. Can you believe the great Jake Sherman is scared about going away to camp for the first time?"

"Am not," I said.

"Are too," she shot back. "I know you, Jake. You're totally freaked."

"I don't see why he should be scared," Mom said. "After all, he's only going for a month and his two best friends will be there with him."

"But Camp Walton has a rule against friends sharing bunks," Jessica said. "Jake's little play pals Josh and Andy will be in other cabins."

"But they'll be at the same camp," Dad said. "They'll get to see each other."

"Doesn't matter," my sister said. "What matters is who Jake shares his cabin with. What happens when they find out what a dork he is? What if they all hate him?"

"Hon?" said my mother to my sister.

"You guys never went to camp when you were kids," Jessica went on. "You don't have a clue how scary going for the first time can be. I mean, knowing Jake, he'll probably do something really dumb on the first day. What if he comes off looking like a fool? Once he's got that label, he's finished. Believe me, I'd be freaked too if I were Jake. This could turn out to be the worst summer of his life."

"*Ahem!*" Mom cleared her throat loudly. "Are you *sure* Jake needs to hear this?"

"Absolutely," Jessica insisted. "Don't you remember what happened to me on my first day at camp? I tripped during a ball game and got a face full of mud. For the rest of the summer they called me Mud Face. It was a total bummer. I hated it. If you ask me, I don't even know why they call it summer *camp*. Summer *prison* is more like it. It can be pure tor — "

"*Hon!*" Mom blurted. "Please stop now. You're scaring Jake."

Jessica blinked and looked surprised.

"Yeah," I said. "What do you want me to do? Stay home with you?"

Jessica's eyes widened. "No!"

Mom smiled. "I think Jessica just got a little carried away. I'm sure this is going to be a great month for Jake."

"It's definitely going to be a great month for *me* without my skinkbrain brother around," said Jessica.

"You may be surprised," said Mom. "You may actually discover you miss Jake."

"Right." Jessica smirked. "I may also discover that I have an extra eye growing out the back of my head and that I love eating chocolate-covered cockroaches, but somehow I doubt it."

My sister was going to spend the summer at the town pool being a junior lifeguard, whatever that meant.

"Listen, guys," I said. "I'm sure everything's going to be cool at Camp Walton, and I'm gonna have a great time."

"That's the spirit." Mom gave me an encouraging smile.

"Just remember, Jake," said my father, "even if you're completely miserable and unhappy, you have to stay. After the first week, they don't give refunds if you leave early. So no matter how bad it gets, you're stuck there."

Mom sighed at Dad. "I know you mean well, dear, but I'm not sure that's the most positive approach to take."

"Look, Mom, Dad," I said. "It really doesn't matter. I — "

Ding dong! The doorbell rang.

Groof! Groof! Lance, our yellow Labrador retriever, started barking.

Jessica got up, went to the kitchen window, and looked outside. "Oh, my gosh! You're not going to believe this!"

2

I went to the kitchen window. Outside my friends Alex Silver, Julia Saks, and Amber Sweeny were standing on the sidewalk in front of our house. They were holding up a large banner made out of a bed sheet. The banner said:

> HAVE A GREAT TIME AT CAMP
> Don't come
> ~~HURRY~~ BACK

"I guess I'm not the only one who's *not* going to miss you," Jessica quipped.

"You're a real riot, Jess," I grumbled, and went to the front door.

As soon as I stepped outside, my friends reached into their pockets and pulled out giant handkerchiefs they must have torn from another sheet. They pretended to cry and blow their noses.

"Gee, guys," I said. "I didn't know you cared."

"We don't," Alex said as he dabbed his eyes. "It must be an allergy or something."

Julia handed me a shoe box. "We took up a collection and got this for you."

"What is it?" I asked.

"A survival kit," said Amber.

I opened the box. Inside was a bag of party balloons, a can of Cheese Whiz, a pack of crackers, and a small box of Band Aids.

"I can understand the Cheese Whiz, crackers, and Band Aids," I said. "But what's with the balloons?"

"You can't survive camp without them," said Alex.

"What are you talking about?" I said.

"Balloons are an essential component in the manufacture of water balloons," he explained. "Camp without water balloons is like a Big Mac without fries."

"Thanks, I'll remember that." I slid the box under my arm. "You guys sure know how to make a kid feel good."

"So when do you leave?" Julia asked.

I checked my watch. "Any minute now."

Amber pointed at my T-shirt. "It's really called Camp Walton?"

"No," I said. "It's called Camp Big-Chewy-Booger but they ran out of those T-shirts so I have to wear this."

Julia and Amber grinned, but Alex had a

pained expression on his face. "Seriously, Jake, what do you want to go to camp for?"

"I guess because I've never tried it," I said.

"You've never tried bungee jumping off the Golden Gate Bridge either," said Amber. "You gonna try that next?"

"Probably not," I said.

"So what are we supposed to do for the next month while you're gone?" Alex asked.

"Uh . . . sit around and miss me?" I suggested.

"Fat chance." Julia smirked.

"Just remember, dude," Alex said. "New experiences can be dangerous. Look what happened to Icarus."

Amber frowned. "*Who?*"

"Don't you remember that Greek dude who made wings out of wax?" Alex asked. "He flew too close to the sun and the wax melted and he fell back to earth and did the big splat."

"If I make any wax wings in arts and crafts, I'll remember not to fly too close to the sun," I said.

Just then Dad, Mom, and Jessica came out.

"Time to go, Jake," said my father as he lugged my big green duffle bag to our van and dumped it in the back. The rear of the van dipped and the springs squeaked. Then Mom and Jessica got in.

My friends grew silent. It was time for me to leave. Suddenly I actually did start to feel a little nervous. Then I had an idea.

"Hey, you guys want to come with us to the

place where the camp bus picks me up?" I asked.

"Not exactly the most exciting offer we've ever had," Alex muttered.

"Where it is, anyway?" asked Amber.

"The parking lot of Super Donut," I said.

"Would your parents get us some donuts if we went?" Julia asked.

"Uhh . . . I don't see why not," I said.

My friends started to grin.

"Suddenly I want to be with Jake until the very last second," said Alex.

"Wait, Jake." My father rolled down his window and stuck his head out. "Don't forget we have to pick up Josh and Andy and all their stuff. That won't leave much room."

"Aw, darn, and I thought we were going to get something good out of this," Julia said with a sigh.

"Sorry, guys." I waved at my friends and got into the van. "Guess I'll see you when I get back."

3

We picked up Josh and Andy at their houses and threw their duffle bags in the van. My friends and I sat together in the back. They weren't exactly happy campers.

"I can't believe I'm going to this dumb camp," Josh groaned.

"Yeah," Andy agreed. "I mean, what's wrong with hanging around here and complaining that there's nothing to do? That's what we do *every* summer."

"Look, guys, this could be really good for us," I said.

"Really good for *you*, maybe," Josh grumbled. "Not for me. I'm the chubby kid. You ever notice in every camp movie there's a chubby kid with six candy bars in his pocket who can't make it around the bases without stopping to catch his breath. Well, that's me."

"No way," I said. "You're a good athlete."

"You and Andy know that," said Josh. "But no

one else does. Everyone's gonna look at me and think of the chubby kid in those movies. They're never gonna give me a chance. I never should've told my parents you were going to camp. Then they wouldn't be making me go."

"Yeah." Andy nodded. "This really bites."

"What's *your* problem?" I asked him. "You're not chubby."

"I've got braces," Andy said.

"So?"

"So they're gonna give me a dumb nickname," Andy said. "Everybody gets a nickname in camp. Mine's gonna be something really stupid like railroad lips or terminator teeth."

"You guys worry too much," I said. "Camp Walton's going to be totally cool."

But Andy and Josh didn't look convinced.

"You guys know what a super-wedgy is?" Andy asked.

Josh and I shook our heads. "Never heard of it."

"My cousin told me about it," Andy explained. "They only have them at camps. The camp cabins have rafters. So they take a rope and put one end through your belt. The other end goes over the rafter. Then they haul you up."

"Eww!" Josh winced in imagined pain and reached for the van's door handle. "Forget it, I'm not going."

"Hold it, you guys," I said. "I think you're just

nervous because they won't let us bunk together. But maybe that's good. We're always together, so this'll be different."

"Sure," Josh moaned. "We'll all get super-wedgied in a different cabin."

"I'll tell you what will be different," Andy said in a low voice so my parents and sister wouldn't hear. "Being away from Mr. Dorkson's dumb machine. At least we won't have to worry about switching bodies with anything for a while."

Josh pretended to look surprised. "Gee, Andy, I thought you liked being Jake's dog."

"Very funny," Andy replied sourly.

Just a few months before, Andy and my dog Lance had accidentally switched bodies. Lance, in Andy's body, went to regular school while Andy, in Lance's body, went to obedience school.

"So listen, guys," I said. "Did you get flashlights?"

"Oh, yeah." Josh opened his day pack and took out a long black flashlight. "It's made of aluminum. Not only does it work as a flashlight, but if I run into any bears in the woods, I can whack 'em on the head."

"Cool," I said, getting out my dual action light. "Mine not only has a spotlight. It has a wide-area fluorescent that blinks automatically so that if I get lost in the woods at night a search plane can find me."

We both turned to Andy, to see what kind of

flashlight he'd gotten. Andy opened his day pack and took out a huge thing with a pistol grip and curly black cord leading to a separate battery pack.

"Oh, wow!" I gasped. "That's incredible."

Andy grinned sheepishly. "It's called the SuperBeam. One million candle power. Twenty-five times brighter than the high beams on this van. This thing could light up a whole baseball stadium."

Only Josh didn't look impressed. "It may be bright, but what good is that going to do if you run into a bear?"

"I'll just have to blind him," Andy replied with a smile.

4

The camp bus hadn't arrived yet when we got to the Super Donut. Mom, Dad, and Jessica went inside to buy donuts. Josh, Andy, and I hung out in the parking lot. Josh mumbled something under his breath.

"What?" I didn't quite catch what he'd said.

Josh and Andy winked at each other and grinned.

"What'd you say?" I asked. "I didn't get it."

"I said, 'The fungus says, "What?" ' " Josh spoke more clearly.

"What?" I said.

Josh and Andy grinned some more.

Then I got it and felt my face turn red. "Very funny, guys."

"But you have to admit it's a good one," Andy said.

"Yeah, right." I started to look around, scoping out the other campers.

"Check out those guys." Andy pointed at three

kids throwing a baseball around on the other side of the parking lot. They could all throw really hard and far.

"Serious jock types," Josh said.

"The cool guys," Andy added warily. "Watch out."

"Maybe they're okay," I said.

"Sure, and maybe I'm the frog prince," Andy said. "They're too cool. That's why they're over there throwing the ball around. They want to make sure everyone sees them. You see any parents with them?"

Josh and I shook our heads.

"Of course not," Andy said. "They're letting everyone know that they're too cool to have parents. Not like the rest of us dweebazoids waiting around for the bus with Mom and Dad."

As Andy said that, he pointed at the kids who *were* waiting with their parents. In a weird way it seemed like he was right. The kids who hung with their parents did seem dorkier. Their clothes and hair didn't look as cool.

I looked back at the cool guys. They were definitely wearing the coolest clothes and sneakers, and they had the coolest hair. Then I compared my friends to them. Unfortunately it was hard for Josh to look cool because he was chubby and his face was always red. And Andy rarely looked cool because he had braces and a few zits.

Then I looked down at my own sneakers and clothes. I thought I looked pretty cool too. Could I fit in with those cool guys?

Mom, Dad, and Jessica came out of the Super Donut with three yellow and red travel boxes of donuts.

"There is one *good* thing about parents bringing you to the bus," I said. "They supply the donuts."

"You're right about that," Josh admitted and patted his day pack. "Sure beats Cheese Whiz on crackers."

Andy looked surprised. "You brought that too?"

"So did I," I said.

"It's the universal emergency camp food," said Josh.

My parents and sister arrived with the donuts.

"How come so many boxes, Mrs. Sherman?" Andy asked, eyeing the donuts hungrily.

"We're going to take one box home with us," Mom replied. "The second box we'll eat here, and the third is for Jake to take on the bus and share with all his new friends."

Andy grinned and put his lips close to my ear. *"You're going to share your donuts on the bus,"* he teased. *"Aw, isn't that cute?"*

"Drop dead." I gave him a poke with my elbow.

Meanwhile, Dad opened the first box of donuts. "Come and get 'em, boys."

Josh, Andy, and I each took a donut, then walked a dozen feet away and stood by ourselves.

"Is it my breath?" Dad asked with a concerned look.

As usual, brain-girl Jessica figured out the real reason. "No, Dad, it's Jake. He's afraid that if he stands with his parents he won't look cool to the other kids."

"Then maybe we should go," said Mom.

That made me feel bad.

"Naw, it's okay," I said. "You guys can stay."

"We can stay," said Jessica. "But we're not allowed to get too close to you, right?"

"Right." I nodded.

Jessica rolled her eyes. "Pathetic."

"Oh, look." Mom pointed at a family on the other side of the parking lot. "Isn't that the Peelings?"

We looked across the parking lot at a tall kid with glasses and black hair. He was wearing a white Camp Walton T-shirt and green-and-red-plaid shorts. Some lady, probably his mother, was making him stand still while she reached up and combed his hair.

"You're right," Dad said. "We haven't seen them in years."

"Now that I think of it, they had a boy the same age as Jake," said Mom. "Let's go say hello."

Mom and Dad walked across the parking lot. Meanwhile, the kid's mother was still combing his hair.

"Can you believe she's doing that *in public*?" Andy whispered.

"What's worse is that he's *letting* her do it," Josh added. "That kid must be a triple mega-dorkazoid."

We watched as my parents introduced themselves to the dorkazoid's parents. A few moments later, my mother turned and waved across the parking lot to me. "Jake, hon? Come on over. There's someone here we'd like you to meet."

"Tough break, Jake." Andy grimly clapped his hand on my shoulder. "You just became a dork-azoid by association."

5

As I walked slowly across the parking lot toward my parents and the Peelings, I glanced back at the cool kids playing ball, and hoped they weren't watching. Mr. Peeling was a tall, gawky-looking guy like his son. He had one of the longest necks and the biggest Adam's apple I'd ever seen, and sort of reminded me of a giraffe. Mrs. Peeling was a large woman with a big blond hairdo and lots of jewelry around her neck and wrists. Definitely more of a hippo.

I could just imagine what the son of a giraffe and hippo would be like. Definitely not cool.

"Jake," Mom said, "I want you to meet Mr. and Mrs. Peeling and their son, Peter. They used to be our neighbors in the city. We just found out that you and Peter are both in cabin B-13. Isn't that wonderful?"

Peter held out his hand. It was pretty limp, and he had awful long fingernails for a boy. He didn't look at me when we shook hands.

"Oh, I think this is sooo wonderful!" Mrs. Peeling gushed. "Petey's been sooo worried that he wouldn't know anyone at camp. We had to force him to go. If it was up to him, he'd just sit in front of the TV all day and — "

"Uh, Mom," Peter interrupted. He had a pained look on his face. "I really don't think you have to tell them all that."

"Why not Petey?" his mom asked. "It's true, isn't it?"

Peter's face turned red and I felt bad for him. His mother sure wasn't helping things by embarrassing him like that.

"This is your lucky day, Petey," Mr. Peeling said. "Jake looks like a nice boy. I'm sure you two are going to be best friends by the time camp is over."

An awkward moment passed while neither Peter nor I knew what to say. Just then I happened to look down at his feet. Peter was wearing sandals. He had the longest toenails I'd ever seen.

They were almost lethal weapons!

I straightened up. Peter might have been the greatest guy on earth, but there was no way I was going to be friends with anyone who wore sandals and had killer toenails.

We all heard the squeak of brakes. A green bus pulled into the parking lot. It looked like an old school bus that had been repainted.

"We better go get your stuff, Jake," Dad said. He and Mom said good-bye to the Peelings.

Peter and I just nodded at each other.

"So what do you think of Peter?" Mom asked in a low voice as we walked back across the parking lot to the car.

"I don't know, Mom. He seems a little geeky."

"You'd be geeky too if you had Margaret Peeling for a mother," my father whispered.

"John!" Mom gasped under her breath. "That's not very nice."

"Well, maybe not, but it's the truth, isn't it?" Dad replied with a shrug.

Mom didn't answer. She turned to me. "Well, anyway, Jake. Since he's in the same cabin as you, it would be very nice if you two became friends."

"Sure, Mom," I said. But inside I was thinking, *No way!*

6

We got back to the van. All around us, parents were giving their kids last minute instructions. Or hugging them. Or, in Peter Peeling's case, combing his hair again. The three cool baseball players carried their duffle bags toward the bus. Their parents were nowhere in sight.

Mom spread her arms. "Can I give you a hug and a kiss good-bye, Jake?"

"Uh . . ." I took a step back and looked around, hoping that the cool guys weren't watching.

"Get with the program, Mom." Jessica smirked. "Cool kids don't even *have* mothers. As far as Jake's concerned, you've ceased to *exist.*"

Mom gave me a crooked smile and dropped her arms.

Dad held out his hand. "Then how about a manly shake?"

"Sure." I shook his hand.

"Put 'er there, Jake." Jessica held out her hand. I shook it.

137

Mom sighed and held out her hand as well. "I'm glad we can conclude this meeting in a businesslike manner," she said sarcastically as we shook. "Just don't forget to brush your teeth."

"Sure, Mom."

Josh and Andy had already gotten on the bus. I got my day pack and duffle bag out of the van. The day pack contained my flashlight, Discman, some CDs, and a bag of chips for the bus ride. The duffle bag weighed a ton.

As I trudged toward the bus, almost bent double by the weight of the duffle, Josh opened a window and stuck his head out. "What's in that thing?"

"Don't know. My mom packed it." With a grunt I heaved the duffle bag onto the luggage carrier welded to the back of the bus.

"Better hurry," Josh said. "Looks like you're the last one to get on."

He was right. All the other campers were already on the bus. I spun around to my parents and sister and gave them one last wave. "See you in a month."

"No rush," Jessica called back. She waved with her right hand. Her left hand was behind her back.

I climbed onto the bus. The doors closed behind me and the bus lurched into motion. As I looked out the window, Jessica brought her left hand from behind her back. She held up a red and yellow box of donuts.

My donuts!

Jessica rubbed her stomach and licked her lips. She'd stolen my donuts!

That slimeball!

7

The bus started to move. I was still standing in the front. I looked at the rows of faces in the seats. A lot of the kids were younger, a few were my age and a few were older. Some of them looked back at me. Others gazed out the windows. Still others were already talking to the kid they were sitting next to.

"You better get a seat, son," said an older guy, who was sitting right behind the bus driver. He was wearing glasses, a gray Camp Walton T-shirt, and holding a clipboard.

"Yo, Jake!" About halfway back, Andy waved at me. He was sitting next to Josh. I walked down the aisle toward them. As I got nearer I saw that the closest empty seat was in the row behind them, right next to . . . Peter Peeling.

Dork by association . . . Andy's words echoed in my ears. Part of me said "Don't sit there," but another part of me remembered what Mom had said

140

about being nice. Sitting with the guy on the bus couldn't hurt, could it?

I stopped next to Peter. He looked up at me and smiled a little.

I was just about to sit down in the seat next to him when a voice said, "Look out."

I followed the voice to the back of the bus. The three cool baseball players were sitting in the last row, watching me. They were all wearing headphones, listening to Discmans, and munching on Pringles.

"You really want to sit there?" one of them asked. He was short and stocky, with short black hair and a diamond stud in one ear.

I hesitated and looked down at Peter. He quickly looked away. His ears and cheeks were growing red.

"Hey, it's a free country," said another one of the cool guys in a mocking tone. He was the tallest of the three and had bushy blond hair.

"Yeah, but you gotta watch out for cooties," said the short guy.

The third guy said nothing. His hair was longer and light brown. He was wearing a leather thong around his neck with a single large bead in it.

Andy and Josh twisted around in their seat and looked at me with puzzled expressions.

"Aren't you going to sit?" Andy asked.

"Back there," I answered, and sat down in an

empty row halfway between Peter Peeling and the cool guys.

"Definitely a wise decision," said the short stocky guy with the earring.

"So what's your name?" asked the guy with the longer brown hair and the leather thong.

"Jake," I said. "What's yours?"

"Rick," the kid said.

"Dan," said the stocky kid with the dark hair.

"Zack," said the blond guy. "What cabin you in?"

"B-13," I said. "You?"

"The very same," said Rick, and the other two nodded to show they were in that cabin also.

"Should be a pretty cool group this year," said Dan.

"With one definite exception," added Zack, looking past me at Peter.

8

The bus went over a bump and I felt my eyes open. For a second I didn't know where I was. Then I realized I'd fallen asleep. I yawned and looked out the window. We were pulling into a big gravel parking lot. Other buses were already there and kids wearing white Camp Walton T-shirts were climbing out of them.

In the parking lot, older guys wearing gray Camp Walton T-shirts and carrying clipboards were talking to small groups of campers. In the background were some buildings made of brown logs, and behind them was a lake with a dock and some sailboats.

I rubbed my eyes and stretched.

"Have a nice nap, Sleeping Beauty?" someone asked.

I looked up into Zack's smiling face as he, Dan, and Rick filed down the aisle past me.

"Oh, yeah." I stretched and yawned again.

"See ya in the cabin," said Rick.

A moment later they passed Peter Peeling as he stood up. He picked up a white paper shopping bag that must have contained his bus stuff. The rest of us had day packs. The shopping bag was like Peter — hopelessly dorky.

"Cool bag," Zack said with a chuckle.

Peter didn't reply. He just bowed his head and wouldn't look Zack in the eye. He waited until they left the bus. When they were gone, he went down the aisle and got off.

That left three people on the bus: Josh, Andy, and me.

"How come you didn't sit with us?" Josh asked.

"Uh, well, I knew I was gonna sleep," I lied.

"Bull," Andy said. "You just didn't want to sit next to that Peeling kid. So, did you make friends with the cool guys?"

"Not really," I said, getting up.

"Well, there's still plenty of time," Andy said, as if he could read my mind.

Andy, Josh, and I went down the aisle. Outside the bus, the driver was pulling the duffle bags out of the luggage carrier. Peter Peeling got his bag and spoke to an older guy wearing a grey Camp Walton T-shirt. The guy checked his clipboard, then pointed toward a line of small wooden buildings, which must have been the cabins where we campers would live.

I saw the driver pull out my duffle bag and drop it to the ground with a thud. I went over and struggled to pick it up. Rick, Dan, and Zack were still waiting for theirs.

"What'd you put in there?" Dan, the stocky kid with the black hair, asked with a smile. "Bowling balls?"

I almost answered that I didn't know what was in the bag because my mom had packed for me. But I caught myself. Admitting your mom packed for you wasn't cool.

"I listen to a lot of heavy metal," I said.

Dan scowled, but Rick grinned. He was the one with the brown hair.

"*Heavy* metal?" he said. "That's funny. Are you a comedian?"

"Only when I'm awake," I said.

By now, Andy and Josh had gotten their duffle bags.

"So where's your cabin?" Andy asked me.

I pointed toward B-13.

"Bummer," he said. "Josh and I are that way." He pointed toward some cabins on the other side of a large field with some soccer goals and a base-ball diamond.

"Guess I'll catch you guys later," I said, and started to lug my duffle bag toward my cabin.

Halfway to the cabin, Rick, Dan and Zack passed me. Their duffle bags looked a lot lighter.

"Come on, Sleeping Beauty, don't be such a slowpoke," Zack teased. He was the tall one with the bushy blond hair. I struggled to keep up with them. Ahead we could see Peter Peeling carrying his duffle and white shopping bag. All of a sudden the bottom of the shopping bag split and all the stuff inside spilled onto the grass. Peter dropped his duffle and started to pick up the items, which included a white plastic thing with a long, clear plastic tube attached to it.

Zack, Rick, and Dan paused to watch.

"Hey, guys, look," Zack said. "A Water Pik."

"Whoa." Dan grinned. "This guy takes serious care of his teeth."

"It's for my gums," Peter tried to explain.

"Gums, huh?" chuckled Dan. "Hey, maybe we should call him Gummi Bear."

"Yeah, that sounds right," agreed Zack. He turned to me. "What do *you* think, Sleeping Beauty?"

Suddenly the cool guys and Peter were looking at me, waiting for my reply. Peter winced at the nickname. I could just imagine him writing home and complaining that I'd agreed to call him Gummi Bear. His mother would probably call my mother and scream at her. But I wouldn't have to deal with that until I got home from camp. Right now I was just trying to survive the first fifteen minutes.

"Sounds okay to me." I shrugged and didn't look at Peter.

"So be it," Zack said. "See you in the cabin, *Gummi Bear*."

The cool guys started toward the cabin. I glanced at Peter, but he wouldn't look at me.

"Hey, Sleeping Beauty!" Dan yelled back to me. "You coming or what?"

"Uh, yeah, I'm coming," I said, and followed.

9

Our cabin was pretty small. First you went up two wooden steps to a porch, and then inside through a creaking screen door. Three double decker bunk beds stood in the middle and back. A regular bed was placed near the screen door.

"That's for the counselor," Dan said. "We get the double deckers."

Thunk! I dropped my duffle bag next to the first double decker I came to.

"You don't want to take that one, Sleeping Beauty," Zack said. "Only the dweebs want to be close to the counselor."

"Come on back here with us," said Rick. "You can take the top of my bunk."

I dragged my duffle bag back to Rick's bunk bed and started to unpack. The bunks had thin mattresses, made up with white sheets and gray blankets.

The next camper to enter the cabin was Peter,

who put his stuff down on the bunk nearest the counselor's bed.

"It never fails," Zack said in a low voice. Dan smiled.

The last kid in the cabin was small and blond with a slight build. The only bed left was the top of Peter's double decker, and without a word the blond kid took it.

"It never fails?" Dan said it like a question this time and looked at Zack. I knew he was asking if Zack thought the blond kid was a dweeb, too. I was starting to get the feeling that Zack was the ringleader.

"Looks like it," Zack replied. He looked at me. "What do *you* think, Sleeping Beauty?"

Every time they spoke to me, I felt like I was being tested. Part of me thought it was stupid, but another part of me really wanted to pass the test.

"It's your call," I said with a shrug.

It took a while to get everything unpacked. The reason my duffle bag was so heavy was that my mother had packed enough underwear for me to change four times a day for a month and still have some left over.

While I shoved underwear in my cubby, the cool guys asked where I was from and I asked where they were from. But there was another question I really wanted to ask. Finally I got up the nerve.

"It seems like you guys are pretty good friends," I said. "I thought they had a rule against friends sharing cabins."

"It's not a real firm rule," Zack said. "If you get your parents to write a letter saying you might not come back if you can't be with your friends, the camp overlooks it really fast."

I wished I'd known that sooner. I would have given anything to be with Josh and Andy. Then I wouldn't have to worry about making new friends or being singled out as a dweeb.

A tall, lanky older guy with curly black hair came in. He was wearing a gray Camp Walton T-shirt, and said his name was Marty and that he was our counselor. He had an easygoing smile and looked pretty friendly. But when he focused on Zack, Dan, and Rick his expression changed.

"Don't I remember you three from last year?" Marty asked. "Didn't you three bunk together?"

"So?" Zack asked back.

It looked like Marty was going to say something, but he just shrugged and told the rest of us to introduce ourselves. That's how I found out the small blond kid's name was Lewis.

Marty showed us how the cabin worked. Outside was a clothesline where we could hang our wet bathing suits and damp towels to dry, and in back of the cabin was a hose for washing down our tennis shoes and anything else that got muddy.

Then Marty said he had to go down to the waterfront because he was also one of the swimming instructors. He said he'd come back later and take us over to the cafeteria for lunch. In the meantime we should finish unpacking and get to know each other. He added that there was a new tetherball game in the front of the cabin and we could play if we wanted.

After Marty left, Zack strolled to the front of the cabin and looked up at Lewis. The small blond kid was kneeling on his bunk, tacking pictures of racing cars to a rafter over his bed.

"Guess you're into cars, huh?" Zack asked.

Lewis nodded.

"*Small* cars, right?" Zack said.

"*Fast* cars," Lewis replied.

"*Small* fast cars, then," said Zack with a grin.

In the back of the cabin Dan snickered.

Lewis looked down at Zack, right into his eyes. "You think you're funny?"

Zack blinked. Lewis was challenging him, which was kind of interesting considering Zack was at least eight inches taller and probably weighed forty pounds more.

"Whoa, tough little guy," Dan said in a low voice.

"Mighty Mouse," said Zack with a smile. "Yeah, that's what we're gonna call you. So we got

Mighty Mouse and Gummi Bear in the first bunk."

Lewis turned back to his pictures and didn't say a word. Meanwhile, Peter had been sitting on the lower bunk, quietly unpacking his stuff.

Now Zack turned to him. "Hey, Gummi Bear, wanna play some tetherball?"

Every time one of the cool guys spoke to Peter, he seemed to shiver slightly. He always bowed his head, and never looked them in the eye.

"Uh, I'm not sure."

Zack put his hands on his hips. "What are you, some kind of wuss?"

In the back, Dan snickered again. I noticed that Rick was silent and didn't join his friends when they picked on kids.

"I . . . I don't know what tetherball is," Peter said.

"How can you not know what tetherball is?" Zack asked in disbelief.

"Maybe they don't have it where he comes from," Rick said.

"Well, I'll show you," Zack said.

Peter's eyes darted around nervously. It was obvious he didn't want to play. "Uh, well, I haven't finished unpacking. Marty said we had to finish unpacking before we — "

"What's wrong with you?" Zack asked sharply. "You gonna listen to *everything* your counselor tells you?"

"Well — " Peter stammered.

"Bet I could beat you with one hand behind my back," Zack sneered.

"And on one foot," Dan added.

"Yeah," said Zack. "So how about it, Gummi Bear? Or do we have to start calling you Gummi *Chicken*?"

10

Peter, Zack, Dan, Rick, and I went out to the tetherball court. Lewis, still in the cabin, didn't seem interested in watching the game.

The ball was about the size of a volleyball. It was attached to a rope, and the other end of the rope was attached to the top of a tall metal pole stuck in the ground. The idea was to hit the ball with your fist and make it go around the pole while your opponent tried to make it go in the opposite direction.

Peter and Zack got into position around the tetherball pole.

"You start, Gummi Bear," Zack said, swinging the ball to Peter. Then Zack put his left hand behind his back and raised his left foot off the ground so that he was standing on one foot.

Peter punched the ball. As it swung around the pole, Zack launched himself in the air and belted it with all his might. *Whap!* The ball whipped back around the pole so fast that Peter just barely managed to duck out of the way. As the ball sailed back to Zack, he smacked it again, and then again. The ball rocketed around the pole and reached the end of the tether in no time.

Zack won on one foot with one hand behind his back.

Except for the first time he hit it, Peter never touched the ball again.

Zack grinned triumphantly. Peter trudged into the cabin with his head hanging. Zack had made him look really bad.

"What a dweeb," Dan muttered contemptuously. "And did you see those toenails?"

Zack nodded. "The guy's hopeless." Then he focused on me. "How about *you*, Sleeping Beauty? Think *you* can beat me?"

11

I didn't really want to play Zack and lose. But losing would be better than chickening out. Then again, I didn't want to lose the way Peter lost — never even touching the ball. That wasn't any good either because it would make me look like a wuss. So not only would I have to play, but I'd have to put my body between Zack and the ball, which might cause serious damage to my head.

Given a choice between suffering serious damage to my head or being labeled a chicken wuss, I had to go with the damage.

Taking a deep breath and bracing myself to the prospect of impending pain, I stepped up to the tetherball.

Then I picked up my left leg and put my left arm behind my back. My heart was pounding and my mouth felt dry.

"Whoa!" Rick grinned.

"You don't have to do that," said Zack.

"Hey, I just want to give you an even chance," I replied with a smile.

"All right!" Rick laughed. "This guy's got guts."

"He's still gonna get obliterated," said Dan.

Zack squinted at me, as if wondering if I was really a threat. Then he grinned. "Okay, wise guy, you start."

I steadied the ball with my right hand and prepared to punch it. In my mind was a vision of the ball streaking back at me at supersonic speed and knocking me out cold.

"Hey, guys, time for lunch," someone said. We turned and saw our counselor, Marty, coming toward us. "Where are the others?"

"Still in the cabin," I replied, glad to get out of playing Zack in one-handed, one-footed tetherball.

A few moments later we all started walking toward the dining hall. As I walked with Zack, Rick, and Dan, I noticed that Lewis and Peter followed a dozen yards behind, talking quietly.

What could they be talking about? I wondered. Was Lewis advising Peter to stand up to Zack the way he had?

Meanwhile, the cool guys were also talking quietly.

"You bring the plastic wrap?" Zack asked Dan in a low voice.

157

"Got it right here." Dan patted his pocket. "Who're we gonna do it to?"

"Guess?" Zack jerked his head back toward Peter.

"Who's gonna do it?" Dan asked.

Zack's eyes settled on me. "Sleeping Beauty, who else?"

12

The dining hall was in a big log cabin with a low ceiling. It was noisy and crowded. I spotted Josh and Andy, and we met to compare notes.

"How's your cabin?" I asked Josh.

"Okay," he said with a shrug.

"What about yours?" Andy asked me. "How's it going with the cool guys and Peter the dork?"

"They're really giving him grief," I said.

"You standing up for him?" Andy asked.

"Well, er . . ."

"Forget I even asked." Andy shook his head with disgust. "You're probably too worried about being labeled a dork yourself."

Just then a portly, bald man wearing a gray Camp Walton T-shirt picked up a microphone and told us all to sit. I went back to the table where the guys from B-13 were sitting. The only seat left was next to Peter. Marty sat on Peter's other side and Lewis was sitting across from him.

The portly man's name was Mr. Maller. He was

the owner of the camp. Over the microphone, he told how glad he was that we were all there, how much fun we'd have, and what a big happy family we'd be.

Peter had twisted around in his seat to listen.

Under the table, Zack slipped something into my hand. It was a round piece of plastic wrap.

"Put it over Gummi Bear's glass," he whispered.

It didn't even occur to me to refuse. I reached over and silently stretched the plastic wrap over the top of Peter's glass.

"Make it really smooth so he doesn't notice," Dan added in a hushed voice.

When I was finished, I looked up and straight into the eyes of Lewis, who'd watched the whole thing. I waited for him to say something, or even tell Peter what I'd done. But he just gave me an inscrutable look, and then looked away.

When Mr. Maller's welcoming speech ended, everyone turned back to the table. The camp waiters were coming out of the kitchen with big trays of food. Meanwhile, Zack reached for a metal pitcher in the middle of the table. "Who wants bug juice?"

"Me, me, me, me." Everyone at the table said they wanted some.

"Here you go." Zack stood up and poured out the bug juice. He held the pitcher high so that a

160

long red stream cascaded out and into each glass.

Finally every glass except Peter's was filled.

"So, Gummi Bear, you sure you want some?" Zack asked.

Peter nodded.

"Bombs away." Zack poured.

The red bug juice hit the plastic wrap over Peter's glass and splattered in every direction. Most of it landed on Peter's T-shirt. The rest dripped off the table and into his lap, staining his shorts.

In no time Peter's clothes were drenched in red.

"Gee, how'd that happen?" Zack scratched his head and pretended to be puzzled.

Peter looked down at the plastic-covered glass, and then at Marty, our counselor, sitting on his left. Then he looked at Lewis sitting across from him. Then at me, sitting on his right. We were the closest to him, so it made sense that one of us had put the plastic wrap on his glass.

Obviously Marty wouldn't have done it, and Peter had already made friends with Lewis. Peter's eyes stopped on me, and he stared with a hurt, defeated expression.

He knew I'd done it.

13

Peter went back to the cabin to change his clothes.

Marty gave Zack and Dan a stern look. "Yeah, now I remember. You guys really caused grief in your cabin last year. I'm surprised they let you bunk together again this year."

"Must've been a clerical error," Zack said with a shrug.

"Yeah, right." Marty wasn't fooled. "Try to give Peter a break, okay? You guys can all have a fine time this month without making him miserable, understand?"

We all nodded somberly. But when Marty looked away, Zack cracked a smile and winked.

The waiters served us lunch. Everyone stared down at their plates, but nobody lifted a fork. It was hard to tell exactly what lunch was. It was a glob of red and yellow with bits of green. Looking closely I identified noodles, cheese, and tomato sauce.

"Oh, man, not on the first day," Marty groaned, pressing his face into his hands.

"Yeah, this is no fair," Dan agreed. "They usually wait a few weeks before they hit us with this."

"What is it?" I asked.

"They call it American Chop Suey," Marty said unhappily. "Macaroni and cheese, broccoli, and whatever else happens to be lying around in the kitchen. Then they drown the whole thing in tomato sauce. Don't get the wrong idea, guys. This is a good camp. But the food stinks."

Nobody took more than two bites of the stuff. Lunch became bread, bug juice, and ice cream for dessert. I could have killed Jessica for stealing my donuts.

Afterwards, Marty gave us a tour of the camp, showing us the sports fields, the waterfront, and where the nature walk began. Then we had free time until dinner. Peter and Lewis went their separate ways. I found myself at the basketball court with Rick, Zack, and Dan.

Zack put his hands on his hips and looked around. "Too bad Gummi Bear's not here. It would be kind of fun to play some ball with him. Anyone know where he went?"

"I thought he said something about the nature walk," Rick said.

Zack grinned. "Figures. What about Mighty Mouse?"

"The waterfront," said Dan.

"Why don't the four of us play?" Rick suggested. "We can play two-on-two."

"You play B-ball, Sleeping Beauty?" Zack asked.

"A little," I replied cautiously.

"A little, huh?" Zack said. "Well, then you can be on Rick's team."

So Rick and I teamed up against Dan and Zack to play 21. We played half-court and the game stayed pretty close. Zack was a good basketball player, but Dan wasn't. Rick and I were a more balanced team.

Soon the score was tied 20–20. We were breathing hard. Our wet T-shirts clung to our sweaty bodies and our hair was plastered down with perspiration.

"Next basket wins," Rick reminded us.

Zack paused for a moment and whispered something in Dan's ear.

"Watch out," Rick cautioned me in a low voice. "They're cooking up a plan."

Dan started with the ball and I covered him. Somewhere behind me I could hear the scrape of basketball shoes against the pavement as Zack and Rick jockeyed for position.

Dan drove to my right. As soon as I started to follow, I tripped over something.

The next thing I knew, I was falling.

Wham! I hit the ground, scraping my hands

and knees on the asphalt. Now I knew what had happened. Zack had stuck out his leg so that when Dan started his drive, I'd trip.

Meanwhile Zack spun around and took a pass from Dan. He went in for an easy lay-up and won the game.

"All right!" He and Dan shared a triumphant high five. They were both grinning.

I got up and dusted the dirt off my hands. "Nice trip, Zack."

The smile slowly disappeared from Zack's face. "What'd you say, Sleeping Beauty?"

"You tripped me," I said.

"I did not," Zack said. "You fell."

"Give me a break." I rolled my eyes.

Zack's eyes became beady. "What are you gonna do about it? Go cry to Marty like Gummi Bear would?"

"No," I said.

Zack grinned like he knew he had me, then turned away. It made me mad.

"The cretin says, 'What?' " I muttered in a low voice.

"What?" Zack stopped and looked back at me. The lines between his eyes made a deep V.

Rick grinned. I could see he got it.

"Nothing," I said.

Zack turned away. "Come on, guys," he said to Dan and Rick. "Let's go."

Dan quickly started toward the cabin with

Zack, but Rick stayed behind.

"Hey, come on," he said to me. "It was just a game."

I was still ticked off, but I realized what Rick was doing. He was giving me the chance to keep hanging with the cool guys. I couldn't say no.

14

Everybody met at the cabin before dinner. After the basketball game I was feeling pretty ripe, so I took a shower. When I came out of the bathroom, Zack had taken off his shirt and draped a towel over his shoulder. I figured he was waiting to take a shower next. In the meantime, he was giving Peter grief again.

"You went on the *nature walk*?" Zack made a face. "What are you, some kind of freak?"

Peter bowed his head and stared at the floor.

"Hey, Zack . . ." Rick started to say.

"Yeah, what?" Zack snapped.

"Maybe you should leave the guy alone," Rick said.

"Guy?" Zack stared straight at Peter. "I don't see a guy. I don't know what I see. It's like something from another planet."

Rick didn't answer. For some reason he looked at me.

"The dirtbag says, 'What?' " I muttered.

Zack spun toward me. "What?"

"Shower's free," I said.

Zack forgot about Peter and went into the bathroom. I caught Rick's eye. He winked.

That night after dinner they were showing *Star Wars* in the dining hall. In the cabin before the movie, I saw Zack and Dan talking in low voices and knew they were planning something. Then Dan went into the bathroom.

"Everyone ready?" Marty asked.

"Dan's in the bathroom," Zack said.

"Okay, we'll wait," Marty said.

Dan took forever. After a while, Marty got impatient and walked to the back of the cabin.

"Hey, Dan, you okay?" he called into the bathroom.

"Yeah, I'll be out in a second," Dan called back.

"You sure you're not lost?" Zack yelled and everyone laughed. That was the thing about Zack. Not only was he cool and a good athlete, but he could be funny too.

When he wasn't being mean.

Dan finally got out of the bathroom and we headed toward the dining hall. I was looking forward to sitting with Josh and Andy, but when we got there it was dark inside. The movie had already started.

"Looks like we'll have to sit in the last row," Marty said in a hushed voice.

I had a feeling Zack and Dan had planned it that way. In the meantime, Marty didn't sit down with us.

"Okay, guys, you stay here and watch," he whispered. "I'll be back just before the movie's over." Then he left.

"Where's he going?" I whispered to Rick.

"Probably to hook up with the other counselors and figure out how to meet the counselors from the girls' camp across the lake," Rick whispered back.

We started to watch *Star Wars*, even though you had to assume every camper there had already seen it about a hundred times. After about ten minutes, I felt someone nudge my shoulder. Looking over, I saw Zack, Dan, and Rick sliding out of our row.

"You coming?" Zack whispered.

I hesitated. Marty had told us not to leave the movie.

But if I didn't . . . I was a dweeb.

I didn't ask any questions as we walked through the moonlight back toward the cabin. Crickets chirped in the dark and the night air was fresh and cool. Inside the cabin it was dark, but just enough moonlight came through the windows to allow us to see.

"No lights, guys," Zack whispered, then turned to me. "Hey, Sleeping Beauty, you know how to short-sheet a bed?"

I shook my head.

"Show him, Rick," Zack said as he picked up Peter's Water Pik and shined a small pencil flashlight on it.

Rick pulled the blanket off Peter's bed and started to show me what to do. "See, you double the sheet up short," he said. "Then the guy gets in and can't get his legs straight. We do it to everybody at least once. It's pretty harmless."

"What about Mighty Mouse?" Dan asked.

Zack looked up from the Water Pik and thought for a second. He shook his head. "Let's just do Gummi Bear tonight. Dan, you pull his springs."

While Rick and I doubled over the sheet so that it only went halfway down the bed, Dan crawled underneath. I heard the scrape and squeak of metal as he pulled out some of the springs that supported the mattress. Meanwhile, Zack got a small bottle of liquid detergent and poured it inside the Water Pik.

Dan crawled out from under Peter's bed with a handful of large gray springs. "Man, this is gonna be great! I bet Gummi Bear'll be packed up and gone by the morning."

Rick and I looked at each other. I wondered what he was thinking. Was the point to make Peter so miserable that he'd leave camp?

Rick and I finished. The truth was, I didn't feel good about doing it. Short-sheeting the bed might not be so bad. But the stuff Zack and Dan were doing was mean. Still, I was certain I'd be labeled a geek if I didn't go along with them. And then Zack might start goofing on me, too.

"What else can we do to Gummi Bear?" Dan asked.

Zack started to look around the cabin. But just then Rick walked to the door and peaked out.

"Hey, you hear that?" he whispered to us.

"What?" Zack whispered back.

"I think someone's coming!" Rick hissed.

Everyone froze. Zack tiptoed to the door and looked out. "I don't see anyone," he said in a low voice.

"Well, I thought I saw someone," Rick whispered.

Zack turned back to Dan and me. "Okay, guys, we better get back to the movie."

We quietly snuck out into the dark. No one was outside. I started to wonder if Rick had really seen someone or not. Or was that just his way of stopping Zack and Dan from doing anything more to Peter?

15

We snuck back into the dining hall and watched the end of the movie. Just before the lights went on, Marty rejoined us.

"Okay, guys," he said as the lights went back on, "what do you say we hit the canteen and then head back to the cabin?"

We walked over to the canteen, which was mobbed with campers who had the same idea as us. We got our ice cream, then I spotted Josh and Andy in the crowd and joined them.

"Hey, it's the cool guy," Josh said when he saw me.

"What are you talking about?" I asked.

"We heard about that stunt you pulled on Peter at lunch," Andy said. "You're just too cool for words, Jake."

"Yeah, you're our hero," Josh said snidely.

"Look, forget about it, okay?" I said. "I didn't know he was going to get splattered with bug juice. And anyway, I thought you guys said Peter was a dork."

"Maybe he is," said Andy. "But we wouldn't go out of our way to make his life miserable."

"Not like *someone* we know," added Josh.

"Okay, okay, I get the message," I said. "But how's it going with you guys? Meet anyone in your cabins that you like?"

Andy shrugged his shoulders. "I've spotted a few possible candidates, but I'm taking my time."

"I found a kid in my cabin I like," Josh said. "He's an overweight tubazoid like me. I figure we'll stick together and fight off the cool guys who try to pick on us."

His words stung.

"And speaking of cool guys, how's it going with *you*?" Andy asked.

"All I'm doing is trying to get by, okay?" I said, feeling defensive. "No one wants to be labeled a dork, right?"

"Sure, Jake," Andy said. "Just don't forget, when in doubt, always pick on someone dorkier than you."

I left them and rejoined Marty and the guys, who were walking back to the cabin with their ice creams. Talk about a shock — Zack was having a friendly chat with Peter!

"So, do they call tetherball something else where you come from?" Zack asked.

"Not really," replied Peter. "It never had a name. It was just the game with the ball on the rope. Like soap on a rope."

"Like soap on a rope!" Zack grinned. "That's a good one, Peter."

Peter smiled proudly. He was probably feeling really good because it looked like the cool guys were finally accepting him.

Of course, he didn't know what lay ahead.

16

We got back to the cabin and Marty told us to get ready for bed. Zack had already warned us to stall so that Peter would be the first to use the bathroom.

The rest of us pretended to be busy. Peter was humming to himself, obviously in a good mood. Probably because he thought the cool guys liked him and camp wouldn't be so bad after all. Finally, he got his Water Pik and went into the bathroom. Zack quickly motioned for us to follow.

We couldn't get too close because Peter would see us in the mirror, so we huddled outside the bathroom and listened.

The Water Pik started to whir. Peter was still humming to himself. The humming and whirring sort of mixed together as he started to clean his teeth. But they were quickly joined by a third *spritzing* sound. Like whipped cream squirting out of a can.

"Huh? Wha . . . ?" Peter sounded like he was

trying to talk through a mouthful of food. We heard him spit and gasp, "Hey! What's going on?"

I felt someone prod me from behind. It was Zack, pushing us into the bathroom. Peter saw us in the mirror and spun around. His mouth was covered with foam and it dribbled down his chin. Meanwhile, the Water Pik was spitting out a thin stream of foam over everything in sight!

Zack and Dan started falling all over themselves with laughter. Rick and I were more restrained, but we had to grin. It was a pretty funny sight.

The lines in Peter's forehead deepened as he wiped the foam away from his mouth. His dream of a great month of summer camp was going up in smoke.

Then Marty came into the bathroom. Everyone tensed as we waited to see how he'd react.

When our counselor saw what happened he just shook his head and smiled. "Don't worry, Peter. It's a practical joke. We always get them on the first day. But that's the end of it, right, Zack?"

"Sure, dude, we were just fooling around." Zack patted Peter on the back. A small smile appeared on Peter's face as he tried to laugh along with everyone else. Meanwhile, Marty turned to Zack. "Okay, guys, enough funny stuff. Let's get to bed."

We drifted back to our bunks. Peter stayed in the bathroom to rinse the detergent out of the

Water Pik. Then he came out. We all watched as he pulled back his blanket and hopped into bed.

Ripppp! Peter's eyes went wide and his jaw dropped. With those long toenails, his feet must've torn right through the sheet!

Creak! Before he had time to react, the bottom of the bed parted where Dan had pulled out the springs.

Thwamp! Peter and his mattress sank through the opening and settled on the floor.

"Hey!" Peter struggled to get out of the bed. The mattress had closed around him like a glove. His arms and legs waved wildly like a beetle who'd been turned upside down. No matter how hard he tried, he couldn't get enough of a grip to lift himself out.

Meanwhile, Dan and Zack were doubled over with laughter. But this time, Marty didn't smile as he helped Peter out of his bed. As soon as Peter was on his feet, he bolted out the screen door and disappeared outside.

Marty glared at us angrily, then followed Peter into the dark.

17

We waited around in the cabin for Marty and Peter to come back. Dan chewed nervously on his fingernails and toyed with his diamond stud earring.

"Maybe we went too far, Zack," he said.

Zack smirked and pushed his fingers through his bushy blond hair. "What can they do? Throw all four of us out of camp on the first day? Forget it. Our parents would all ask for refunds. Old Man Maller's too tight to give back a cent."

"You think Peter'll come back?" Rick asked.

"I hope not," Zack said. "You really want a geek like that in our cabin?"

Rick and I exchanged another look. I got the feeling he didn't feel any better about what just happened than I did. But if we both felt that way, how come we couldn't stand up to Zack and tell him to lay off Peter?

We waited. The only sound in the cabin was

that kid Lewis, lying on the bunk above Peter's, slowly thumbing through a car magazine.

After a while, Marty came back. The corners of his mouth curled down. "Congratulations, guys, you've probably ruined Peter's summer."

"It was just a joke," Zack said with a shrug.

"No, it wasn't *just* a joke," Marty replied angrily. "It was too many jokes and all aimed at the same kid. After a while it changes from a joke to a message. And Peter heard it loud and clear."

"So where is he?" Rick asked.

"He's staying in another cabin tonight," Marty said. "Right now he's determined to leave camp tomorrow. I'm going to see if I can talk him out of it, but I have my doubts." He leveled his gaze at Zack. "Congratulations on a job well done, jerk."

Zack shrugged. Marty got some things out of Peter's cubby.

"I'm going to bring him his stuff," he said. "It's way past lights out, so just go to bed. Last guy turns off the lights."

Marty left the cabin again.

"Man, what a dork," Zack muttered.

"Yeah," Dan agreed.

I washed up and climbed into my bunk. The camp pillow was hard and lumpy, and the blanket itched. A few moments later, Rick turned off the lights and walked with his flashlight to the bunk under mine.

179

I lay in the dark feeling really bad. It looked like I'd managed to get in with the cool guys. But in doing so, I'd helped ruin Peter Peeling's summer. And he'd done nothing to deserve it. It wasn't his fault that he was dorky, or that he had an overprotective mother.

I yawned and felt myself growing sleepy. My first day of camp was over. But I knew that if I had it to do all over again, I would do it differently.

18

DAY TWO

The bus went over a bump and I felt my eyes open. Wha . . . ? Where was I?

On a bus?

How?

I sat up straight and looked out the window. The bus was pulling into a big gravel parking lot. Other buses were already there and kids wearing white Camp Walton shirts were climbing out of them.

Wait a minute! I felt a shock race through me. Like being zapped with a cattle prod.

It was the same as yesterday.

Like, been there, done that!

What was going on? Was this a dream?

I sure hoped it was.

I looked a few rows ahead and saw the back of Peter Peeling's head. In the row in front of him, Josh and Andy were getting their things to-gether.

I twisted around. In the back seat, Zack, Dan, and Rick were getting up.

It definitely felt more real than a dream.

"Have a nice nap, Sleeping Beauty?" Zack asked with a grin.

Oh no! This was sounding totally *too* familiar.

"What's the matter?" Zack asked me. "Can't talk?"

"I can talk," I said.

"Good, we were worried there for a moment." Zack smiled as he, Dan, and Rick filed down the aisle past me.

"See ya in the cabin," said Rick.

I watched them go down the aisle. Meanwhile, Peter stood up, clutching his white shopping bag.

"Cool bag," said Zack with a chuckle.

Same as yesterday . . .

I was stuck in the first day of camp!

19

Why me?

I took a deep breath and let it out slowly. Well, maybe I shouldn't have been so surprised.

The reason I wasn't totally instantly freaked out of my skull was that this wasn't the first time it had happened. Last time I'd gotten stuck in the first day of school.

The difference between last time and this time was simple. Last time I didn't know why I'd been stuck in the same day over and over again. This time it was obvious.

Whoever was in charge of these things decided I was going to do the first day over again.

Because of Peter.

In a strange way I was sort of glad, because this time I'd do it right.

I grabbed my day pack and started down the aisle, but when I got to Peter's seat, I stopped.

"Have a good ride?" I asked him. Meanwhile, in

the seat in front of Peter, Andy and Josh swiveled around and watched.

Peter gave me an uncertain look. "Uh, it was okay, I guess."

"I fell asleep," I said. "Was it a long trip?"

"Just a couple of hours," Peter said. "Not too bad."

"Well, come on," I said, hitching my day pack over my shoulder. "We better get off."

"Uh, yeah." If Peter was acting a little wary, it was probably because I'd acted like I didn't want to sit with him before. Of course I couldn't explain why. The only thing I could do was be really friendly now.

Peter and I got off the bus, followed by Josh and Andy. Outside, the driver was pulling the duffle bags out of the luggage carrier. Rick, Dan, and Zack were waiting for theirs.

"There's my duffle," Peter said, and went to get it. That's when I felt a tap on my shoulder. Wheeling around, I found Josh and Andy behind me.

"What's with you?" Josh asked in a low voice.

"What are you talking about?" I played dumb.

"When you got on the bus you acted like you didn't want to sit next to that Peeling kid," Andy said. "Now you're acting like best friends. So, what gives?"

"The reason I didn't sit with him was because

I knew I was gonna sleep," I lied. "I mean, forget what he looks like. The guy's in my cabin and I'm gonna be friendly with him no matter what."

Josh and Andy shared a funny look, but didn't say anything more about it. By then Peter had gotten his duffle bag and was headed toward our cabin.

"I guess our cabins will be up that way, too," Josh said.

"No, you guys are over there." I pointed toward the cabins on the other side of the athletic field.

Andy frowned. "How do you know that?"

"It's weird," I said with a shrug. "I just feel like I've been here before."

I saw the driver pull out my duffle bag and drop it to the ground with a thud near where Zack, Dan, and Rick were standing. I went over and struggled to pick it up.

Dan started to smile.

"No, it's not bowling balls," I said.

He scowled.

By now, Andy and Josh had gotten their duffle bags and spoke to the guy with the clipboard.

Andy turned and looked at me with a puzzled expression. "You were right. Our cabins are over there. How'd you know?"

I was going to explain how I'd seen it all in my crystal ball. But out of the corner of my eye I saw

Peter's white shopping bag split and all his stuff spill out onto the ground.

The cool guys were going to catch up to him any second. I quickly turned back to Andy and Josh.

"Gotta run, dudes," I said.

20

Peter put down his duffle and started to pick up his stuff, including the Water Pik.

"Hey, guys, look," Zack was saying as I caught up to them. "A Water Pik."

"Whoa." Dan grinned. "This guy takes serious care of his teeth."

"It's for my gums," Peter tried to explain.

"Gums, huh?" chuckled Dan. "Hey, maybe we should call him Gummi Bear."

"Yeah, and maybe we should call you Gummi *Brains*," I said.

The cool guys spun around and stared at me. I felt weird. Like in that instant I had just become their enemy.

"Well, look who's here. It's Sleeping Beauty," Zack said. He nudged Dan. "You gonna take that from him?"

Dan narrowed his eyes at me. He was shorter than me, but more powerfully built. I felt my stomach tighten. I didn't want to fight, but I might not have a choice.

"Didn't you say you were in B-13?" Dan asked.

"That's right."

"Better learn to sleep with one eye open," he warned me, then turned to the others. "Come on, guys, let's let these two geeks get to know each other."

Zack and Dan started toward the cabin. Rick gave me a puzzled look, and then followed. I kneeled down with Peter and helped him pick up his stuff.

"Thanks, Jake," he said.

"Hey, always available to help pick stuff up," I said with a grin.

"That's not what I meant," Peter said.

"I know." I winked at him.

Between the two of us, we managed to pick up all his stuff.

"Maybe we'll get lucky and they'll leave us alone," Peter said under his breath as we walked toward the cabin.

"Yeah." I pretended to agree. But knowing Zack, we were going to be anything *but* lucky.

21

We got into the cabin. The cool guys had already staked out the bunks in the back.

Thunk! I dropped my duffle bag next to the first double decker. Standing by his bunk in the back, Zack leveled his gaze at me. I knew what he was going to say.

"It never fails, right?" I said.

Zack blinked as if I'd taken the words out of his mouth.

Peter came in and dropped his duffle bag next to mine. "What never fails?" he asked me in a low voice.

"The jerks take the bunks in the back," I whispered.

Peter grinned.

Just like the day before, Lewis was the last kid in the cabin. This time the only bed left was the top of Rick's double decker.

"Looks like we've got ourselves a real winner cabin this year," Zack muttered.

"Yeah, I wonder if it's too late to get a transfer," Dan replied.

I could have said something, but I decided to keep my mouth shut. There was no sense in asking for trouble. I was pretty sure I was going to have enough of it anyway.

A little later Marty came in and told us all to introduce ourselves. I turned to Peter and told him to come with me.

"Why?" he asked when he saw that I was heading toward the back of the cabin.

"You'll see," I said.

Peter reluctantly followed me. I stopped next to Zack's bunk.

"Listen, Zack," I said. "This is Peter Peeling. And that's what he wants to be called, not Gummi Bear. Our parents were friends when we were little. I haven't seen him in a long time, but he's a good guy."

Zack gave me a blank look. Then a slight smile crept onto his lips. "He can't introduce himself?"

"Well, you guys gave him a pretty hard time before," I said.

"What are you, his bodyguard?" Dan sneered.

"Look, we don't all have to be friends, okay?" I said. "But we do have to live together in this cabin. Now we can either have a good time or a miserable time. It's up to you."

Zack nodded slowly. "Thanks for telling me

that, Sleeping Beauty." Then he offered his hand to Peter. "I'm Zack Zanko."

"Uh, hi," Peter replied and shook his hand.

For a split second I felt pretty good. Like maybe things would work out after all. But then Peter's face turned pale and he started to wince. I looked down at their hands. Zack was squeezing so hard his knuckles had turned white.

"Nice to meet you, Peter," Zack said with an icy grin.

22

After Zack let go of Peter's hand, we went back to unpacking. Marty left for the waterfront and Zack looked up at Lewis, who was kneeling on his bunk, tacking up his car pictures.

"Guess you're into cars, huh?" Zack asked.

Lewis nodded.

"*Small* cars, right?" Zack said.

"*Fast* cars," Lewis replied.

"*Small* fast cars, then," said Zack with a grin.

In the back of the cabin Dan snickered. Hearing it again really made me mad.

"The jerk-magnet says 'What?' " I said in a low voice.

Zack turned and frowned. "What?"

Rick smiled.

"Why do you have to pick on everybody?" I asked Zack.

This time Zack didn't look surprised that I'd interfered. "I wasn't talking to *you*, Sleeping Beauty."

"Well, I'm talking to you," I said, facing him.

"Hey," Lewis said from up on his bunk. Zack and I both looked up at him. Lewis was looking at me. "Thanks, but I can take care of myself."

"Whoa!" Dan chuckled. "Sounds like we got a whole *cabin* full of tough guys."

"Yeah." Zack cracked his knuckles. "Maybe it's time to find out just how tough everyone *really* is."

"Hey, who wants to play that new tetherball game?" Rick suddenly asked.

Zack looked around. "Yeah, sure, let's play." He turned to Peter. "Wanna play some tetherball, Gummi Bear?"

"Uh, I'm not sure," Peter replied nervously.

Zack put his hands on his hips. "What are you, some kind of wuss?"

"No, he's not a wuss," I said. "Not only that, but he'll play you on one foot and with one hand behind his back."

"I will?" Peter asked, bewildered.

Zack scowled, then grinned. "That's just what I was gonna say. Okay, let's do it!"

He, Dan, and Rick went outside. Peter hesitated and looked at me. "What's tetherball?"

"It's the game with the pole and the ball on the rope," I said. "Don't worry, you can do it."

Peter's eyes darted around nervously. "But I haven't finished unpacking. Marty said we had to finish unpacking before we — "

193

"Yeah, I know," I said. "But if you don't go out there and play, Zack is going to give you grief forever. You can finish unpacking later."

Peter winced at the thought of facing Zack in tetherball.

"Go on, Peter," I urged him. "You don't have to beat him, just go out there and show that you're willing to play."

"Aren't you coming?" Peter asked.

"Sure," I said. "I'll be out in a second."

"Promise?" Peter asked.

"Yeah, honest, I promise."

Peter went out the screen door. I looked up at Lewis, who was still tacking car pictures to the rafters.

"Hey, Lewis?" I said.

"Yeah." He paused and looked down at me.

"About what happened before," I said. "The only reason I spoke up against Zack is because I think you, me, and Peter better stick together, okay?"

"Why?" Lewis asked.

"Because I have a feeling those guys are gonna cause a lot of trouble for us," I said.

Lewis gazed past me. It seemed like he was looking out the screen door at the cool guys, who were getting ready to play tetherball. "Thanks, Jake. But like I said before, I can take care of myself."

I left the cabin. Zack, Dan, and Rick were standing by the tetherball court with Peter. Zack was already on one foot, waiting while Peter tried to decide which foot and hand to use. The poor guy was totally uncoordinated. Zack was going to demolish him.

"Hey, wait a minute," I said. "This isn't really fair."

Zack rolled his eyes. "Now what?"

"Well, tetherball is something you're really good at," I said. "So of course you're gonna beat Peter. If he has to play you in tetherball, then you should agree to play him at something he's really good at."

"Okay, sure," Zack said with a sigh. "What'll it be, Gummi Bear?"

"Uh . . ." Peter had to think. "How about Scrabble?"

"Scrabble?" Zack repeated in disbelief. Dan clamped his hand over his mouth to keep from laughing out loud. Even I had to admit it wasn't the best idea.

"Isn't there something else?" I asked Peter. "You know, something you guys can play *outside*?"

Peter bit his lip. "Croquet?"

"You mean, with the wooden balls and the mallets and the wire thingies?" Dan asked.

"They're called wickets," Peter informed him.

"Oh, man." Zack shook his head and groaned. "What a dork!"

Peter gave me a pleading look, like he hoped I'd come to his rescue. I really wanted to, but it wasn't going to be easy.

23

Fortunately, before Zack had a chance to slaughter Peter in one-handed tetherball, Marty arrived and took us to lunch. The cool guys went ahead and Peter and I followed.

"Just my luck," Peter muttered under his breath.

"What do you mean?" I asked.

"I have to get stuck in a cabin with those guys," he said.

"I have a feeling there might be guys like that in *any* cabin," I said.

Peter nodded. "Well, then I guess I'm lucky that we're in this together."

Maybe, I thought.

Once again the dining hall was noisy and crowded with kids. I saw Josh and Andy.

"Catch you later," I said to Peter, planning to go talk to my friends.

"Where're you going?" he asked.

"Uh, just to talk to my friends," I said.

Peter glanced at the table where B-13 sat. The cool guys were already there. He turned to me. "Uh, can I come with you?"

"Hey, don't worry," I said. "I'll be back in a minute."

Peter didn't look happy, but he headed toward the table while I headed toward my friends.

"How's it going with the cool guys and Peter the dork?" Andy asked.

"They're really giving him grief," I said.

"You standing up for him?" Andy asked.

"Better believe it."

Andy and Josh traded an uncertain look.

"You sure that's what you want to do?" Josh asked.

"Hey, someone's got to do it," I said. "Otherwise, the kid's gonna be this summer's sacrificial lamb."

"Yeah, but how about *you*?" Andy asked.

"What about me?" I asked, not understanding what he meant.

"How are you gonna have any fun if you're always defending Peter?" he asked.

Out of the corner of my eye, I saw Mr. Maller, the owner of the camp, walking toward the microphone. I knew I wouldn't have time to explain to my friends that I was trapped in the first day of camp, and that I was pretty certain that the only way I could get out of it was by defending Peter.

"Hey, look, guys," I said. "I'm just trying to do the right thing."

Josh was just about to say something when Mr. Maller got on the microphone and started his speech about how glad he was that we were all there, how much fun we'd have, and what a big happy family we'd be. I said good-bye to my friends, and went back to our table. I sat next to Peter, who had twisted around in his seat to listen to Mr. Maller. Zack and Dan were giving each other looks. Little did they know that I knew what they were planning.

24

Mr. Maller's speech ended, and everyone turned back to the table. The camp waiters were coming out of the kitchen with the trays of American Chop Suey. Zack started to reach for the metal pitcher in the middle of the table, but I grabbed it first and stood up. "Who wants bug juice?"

"Me," Peter said.

I looked down at his glass. It was covered with the plastic wrap. "Oh, gee, your glass has something on it."

Peter stared down at his glass, then removed the plastic wrap. I poured the bright red bug juice.

"Anyone else?" I asked, turning toward the cool guys.

Zack was sitting with his arms crossed, glowering at me. He was obviously mad that I'd foiled his trick.

"I'll have some." Dan held up his glass.

With the pitcher in my hand, I stretched across the table toward him. Unfortunately, I *missed!*

Bright red bug juice splashed all over the table in front of Dan and onto his shirt.

"Hey! What're you doing!" Dan yelled and jumped up.

"Oh, gee, I'm really sorry," I pretended to gasp.

Meanwhile, Zack started to laugh . . . until I *accidentally* spilled bug juice on him too.

"You idiot!" Zack shouted and jumped up. His shirt had a big red stain on it.

"Sorry," I apologized.

"No, you're not!" Zack growled, making a fist. "You did it on purpose!"

The next thing I knew, he started around the table toward me with both hands balled into fists. Luckily for me, Marty got up and blocked his path.

"Chill out, Zack," our counselor said. "Jake said it was an accident."

"Bull," Zack sputtered. "He knew exactly what he was doing. He did it because of the plastic wrap on Gummi Bear's glass. He — "

"That reminds me," Marty said. "Just *how* did the plastic wrap get on Peter's glass?"

Zack suddenly quieted down. He glared past Marty at me. "You're dead meat, Sleeping Beauty."

"Ooh, I'm really scared," I replied.

"Both of you, knock it off," Marty ordered.

"Zack and Dan, go back to the cabin and put on dry clothes. Jake, you promise to be more careful pouring the bug juice next time?"

"You bet." I nodded.

Zack and Dan left. The waiters served lunch and once again we stared at the American Chop Suey in disbelief. I figured the bug juice incident was behind us, so I was surprised when Marty looked up from his plate and said, "Hey, Jake, *did* you do it on purpose?"

"Uh . . ." I didn't know what to say.

"Tell the truth," our counselor said.

"Okay, yeah, I did," I answered.

"Why?" Marty asked.

"Because I don't like the way they pick on Peter," I said.

Marty nodded as if he understood. "No more of that."

25

After lunch, Marty gave us the tour of the camp and then told us we had free time until dinner. I suggested to Peter that we do something together.

"Like what?" he asked.

"I don't know," I said as I watched Rick, Zack, and Dan head for the basketball court. "What do you want to do?"

"Well . . ." Peter scratched his head. "You want to play Scrabble?"

Playing Scrabble was close to the last thing in the world I wanted to do. "Hey, look," I said. "It's a beautiful day. Why don't we do something outside?"

"We could play Scrabble outside," Peter said.

I couldn't help but sigh. I had made it my sworn duty to protect Peter from the cool guys, and make sure he had a decent time at camp. It was the right thing to do. Besides, if I didn't I'd probably be trapped in the first day of camp forever. And if I had to look at American Chop Suey one more time, I was going to barf.

But it wasn't going to be easy to help Peter. The absolute last thing I wanted to do was play Scrabble *outside*. If anyone saw us we'd be labeled super-mega-*quadra*-dorks.

"I really think we should save Scrabble for a rainy day," I said. "Isn't there anything else you'd like to do?"

"Uh . . ." Peter rubbed his chin. "That nature walk sounds pretty interesting."

The nature walk!? Inwardly I groaned. But at least we'd be outside. Besides, I probably wouldn't have to worry about running into anyone I knew. The only guys we'd meet on the nature walk were bound to be dorks.

26

"**W**hat happened to you?" Josh asked when I saw him and Andy outside the dining hall before dinner that night.

"Peter wanted to go on a nature walk," I said, scratching my arm.

"A nature walk?" Andy made a face.

"Hey, it was an educational experience," I said, scratching my ear. "I learned about three different kinds of butterflies, two different kinds of skunk cabbage, a painted turtle, and a red-winged bluebird."

"*Black*bird," Josh corrected me.

"Whatever," I said with a shrug.

Andy studied my face. "I count seven mosquito bites on the left side of your forehead alone."

"The grand body total's somewhere around sixty," I said, scratching my neck. My head, neck, and arms were covered with itching red welts. The nature walk had led Peter and me through a mosquito-infested swamp.

Josh shook his head. "Look, I know you're trying to be a nice guy, Jake. But maybe you ought to spend a little less time with Peter. Not just because everyone's going to think of you as a dork by association, but it's also hazardous to your health."

"I can't," I said.

"Why not?"

I looked around to make sure no one else was listening. Then in a low voice I said, "Because I'm trapped in the first day of camp."

"You're *what?*" Josh's forehead wrinkled.

"I'm trapped in the first day of camp," I said. "Today's the first day of camp for *you*, but for me, yesterday was."

"Yesterday we were back in Jeffersonville," Andy said. "We went Rollerblading, remember?"

"*You* did," I said. "I was here at camp."

"No, you weren't," Josh said. "You were with us."

I shook my head. "Listen, I know this is really hard to explain, but this is the *second* time I've been through this day. Yesterday when we got to camp I tried to be one of the cool guys. I picked on Peter. That was the wrong thing to do so I got punished. They're making me do the day over again."

"Who's making you do it over?" Andy asked.

"I don't know who," I said. "But it's happened to me before. Remember the first day of school last year when Alex Silver decided to be the Knight of Wedgy and wedgy everyone?"

"Oh, yeah." Andy grinned at the memory. "He thought he was so totally cool."

"Well, originally I was into it too," I said. "We were the Knights of Wedgy together. I mean, you have to admit that it feels good to be in with the cool guys."

Andy and Josh both nodded.

"But the thing is," I went on. "If you have to pick on kids to prove you're cool, are you *really* cool? Or are you just some jerk who has to scare kids into thinking he's cool?"

Josh made a funny face. "What does this have to do with going through the first day of camp over again?"

"I had to do the first day of school over about six times before I figured out that being nice to people is better than being mean and cool," I explained. "So now that I'm stuck in the first day of camp I know I have to be really nice to Peter and protect him from the cool guys. Once I've done that, I'll be able to get to the second day of camp."

Josh and Andy shared another doubtful glance.

Then Josh cleared his throat. "I hate to say this, Jake, but are you aware of the fact that you've totally wigged out?"

"Look, it's dumb to argue about this," I said. "You'll never believe me. I probably shouldn't have told you. The weird thing is that it doesn't

207

actually matter. After today everything's going to be normal anyway."

"Except that you and Peter the Geek are joined at the hip," Andy pointed out.

"If Jake really believes this stuff about being trapped in the first day of camp, maybe he *should* be joined with Peter at the hip," Josh said.

"You mean, like two peas in a pod?" Andy asked.

"More like two nuts in a shell," Josh said.

I just smiled. "Whatever you say, guys."

27

After dinner was the movie. I sat on the bench in the back of the dining hall with Peter and the other guys from our cabin. As soon as the movie started, Marty warned us not to get into any trouble, and left. Then the cool guys left.

"Where're they going?" Peter whispered to me.

"Back to the cabin," I whispered back.

"Why?"

"To set booby traps for us."

In the dark, Peter frowned. "How do you know?"

"Trust me," I said in a low voice. "Now listen, I'm gonna leave too. If I don't get back here before the movie ends, tell Marty I had a bad stomachache and went to the nurse."

"Where are you really going?" Peter whispered back.

"I'm going to take care of a few things," I said and started to slide down the bench. Then I stopped and turned back to Peter.

"One last thing," I said. "After the movie you're gonna go get ice cream and Zack's gonna start acting really friendly to you."

"Why?" Peter asked.

"Because he wants to set you up," I explained. "He wants you to think he's going to be your pal so that you won't expect the booby traps. Anyway, when he does it, act like you think he's sincere."

"Why?" Peter asked.

"Because that's how we'll set *him* up," I replied with a wink.

I left the dining hall. Outside the crickets were chirping in the moonlight. Up ahead I could see Zack and his buddies walking quickly back to the cabin. That's where I was headed too, but instead of following them, I snuck around the back of the cabins until I got to B-13.

Standing on my tiptoes behind the cabin I was able to peek in through the screened bathroom window. The cabin was dark and I couldn't see much, but I could hear whispers and the squeak of bedsprings as the cool guys set their traps.

Little did they know that I had a few booby traps of my own to set.

Leaving the back of the cabin, I snuck around the side and found the hose. I brought it around to the front of the cabin and left the nozzle next to the big patch of dirt at the bottom of the front steps. I let the water run slowly and quietly, creating a big mud puddle.

Next I borrowed the clothesline and tied it across the bottom step to the porch, about eight inches from the floor. In the dark, the cool guys would never see it.

Now it was time to sit back and wait.

About fifteen minutes later, the front door of the cabin creaked open and Zack came out, followed by Dan and Rick. Crouching around the side of the cabin, I peeked up and watched.

"Okay, dudes," Zack said as he crossed the porch and started down the front steps. "Let's get back to the . . . *Ahhh!*"

He tripped over the clothesline.

Ker-splat!

Zack fell face-first into the mud puddle.

Up on the porch, Dan looked shocked. Rick had a slight grin on his face. I was starting to wonder whose side that guy was really on.

"What the . . . ?" Zack jumped to his feet in the middle of the puddle. The whole front half of his body was soaked brown with mud. It was in his hair and on his face. His arms and legs were covered.

"Hey, check this out." Dan pointed at the clothesline tied across the bottom step. "Looks like someone booby trapped us while we were booby trapping Gummi Bear."

Zack looked around, fuming. "I bet I know who it was, too."

"So what are you gonna do?" Dan asked.

"I'm gonna take a shower and change my clothes," Zack said. "Then I'm gonna find Sleeping Beauty and destroy him."

28

Rick and Dan headed back to the dining hall. Zack went back into the cabin to change his clothes and clean up. As soon as I heard the shower start to run, I snuck in. The cabin was dark. Only the bathroom light was on. Picking my way around the bunks, I quietly found the pen light in Zack's cubby. Holding the light between my teeth, I pulled every pair of pants and shorts out of his cubby. Then I snuck back out and hid them under the porch.

A couple of minutes later the shower stopped. Zack muttered angrily to himself as he toweled off. He kept grumbling about how he was going to break my skull and make me eat mud. He left the bathroom and headed back to his bunk to put on clean clothes.

"Huh? What the???"

He'd just discovered that he had no pants or shorts. "Oh, man, I'll kill that kid," he muttered.

"Just wait till I find him. I'm gonna break both of his arms."

A few moments later the door of the cabin swung open and slammed closed. From around the corner of the cabin I watched Zack head back toward the dining hall wearing a pair of Dan's shorts all bunched up at the waist.

There was still work to do. Luckily, I had time because the guys were going to go for ice cream after the movie.

I went back into the cabin and found the springs Dan had taken from Peter's and my double-decker bunk. After putting them back where they belonged, I unshort-sheeted our beds and rinsed the detergent out of Peter's Water Pik.

Now it was time to get to work on Zack and Dan's bunk.

29

I was lying on my bed when the cabin door creaked open and Marty came in, followed by the rest of the guys.

"What happened to you?" Marty asked.

"I had a stomachache and went to see the nurse," I said. "I just got back here a few minutes ago."

"Does it still hurt?" he asked.

"Naw, it's a lot better," I said.

Marty told the rest of the guys to get ready for bed. When Zack passed my bunk, he squinted angrily to let me know that I hadn't fooled him. I smiled back.

Just like the night before, the cool guys stalled and pretended to be busy so that Peter would be the first to use the bathroom. Finally, Peter got his Water Pik and went into the bathroom humming to himself. I'd warned him about what was going to happen, so he knew he had to pretend to be in a good mood and act like he thought the cool guys liked him.

As soon as Peter went into the bathroom, Zack quickly motioned for the cool guys to follow. They huddled outside the doorway and listened.

The Water Pik started to whir. Peter was still humming to himself. The humming and whirring mixed together as he started to clean his teeth.

And that's the way it stayed until Peter finished.

Frowning, Zack turned away from the bathroom entrance. Once again, he looked up at me on my bunk and narrowed his eyes. He must've realized that I'd undone his booby traps.

The rest of the guys brushed their teeth and washed up. Then Zack climbed up to his bunk. At the same time, Dan pulled back his blanket and started to get in the bed below.

Sploosh!

Rip!

Zack's mouth fell open. I'd not only short-sheeted his and Dan's beds, I'd added a few water balloons for good measure. He'd not only torn through his sheets, but soaked his mattress as well.

Zack stared daggers at me. "Why you!"

He jumped out of bed, but Marty stepped into his path.

"What's the matter, Zack?" our counselor asked with a smile. "Can't take a joke?"

Zack was seething, balling and unballing his fists, his face red with fury. He just glared past Marty at me and didn't reply.

Dan and Zack went to get new sheets. While they were out Marty talked to me.

"Listen, Jake," he said, barely able to hide his smile. "Let's not have any more of that kind of stuff, okay?"

I nodded, but really got the feeling our counselor was glad that Zack had gotten what he deserved. Peter winked at me and smiled. Lewis looked sort of amused. Rick listened and watched, but said nothing. Still, he didn't look annoyed or anything.

Zack and Dan came back with some towels and dry sheets. They spread the towels over the wet spots on their mattresses, then made their beds with the new sheets and got in.

"Oh, man," Dan moaned. "The water still seeps through."

Zack didn't say anything, but I imagined the water had seeped through his sheets, too.

Marty turned off the cabin lights and told us to go to sleep. I lay in bed in the dark. Despite that hard, lumpy pillow and itchy blanket, I felt pretty good. I'd done the right thing this time. Hopefully with my help, Peter would have a half-decent summer.

And I would get out of being trapped in the first day of camp.

I was just falling asleep when I heard the faintest whisper come from the direction of Zack's bunk. "Hey, Sleeping Beauty."

"What?" I whispered back.

"You better get a good night's rest," Zack whispered. "Because tomorrow you're dead meat."

I rolled over and pulled my pillow over my head so I wouldn't have to listen to any more of his threats.

But it made me wonder.

Maybe I'd made things better for Peter. But I'd also made them pretty bad for me.

Was that the way it *had* to be?

30

DAY THREE

I felt a bump and opened my eyes. Huh? What was I doing on the bus?

It must have been a dream.

I closed my eyes.

Then opened them again.

I was still on the bus.

And it didn't feel like a dream.

This was weird.

Because it *had* to be a dream.

I sat up and looked out the window. We were pulling into the parking lot. The other buses were already there and the new campers wearing white Camp Walton T-shirts were climbing out.

Next I looked inside the bus. Peter was in his seat a few rows ahead. In the row in front of him, Josh was taking off his headphones, and Andy was closing his magazine.

I twisted around. In the backseat, Zack, Dan, and Rick were getting up.

"Have a nice nap, Sleeping Beauty?" Zack asked with a grin.

Uh-oh!

This was no dream!

It was happening again! But why? How was it possible? *I'd done the right thing the day before!*

"What's the matter?" Zack asked. "Can't talk?"

"Uh . . ." I didn't know what to say. I didn't know what to do. I was trapped in the first day of camp again. But it didn't make sense. Hadn't I done what I was supposed to do to get out of this mess?

Why hadn't it worked?

Zack raised an eyebrow. "Is 'uh' all you can say?"

He was waiting for me to say something, but I didn't know what to do. If being friendly didn't work, and being *unfriendly* was no good either, then what was the answer?

I looked up into Zack's face as he, Dan, and Rick filed down the aisle past me. Zack's mouth was a hard, straight line. Dan gave me a curious look.

I stretched and yawned.

"See ya in the cabin," said Rick.

They passed Peter as he stood up with his white paper shopping bag. Zack made his comment about the bag, and Dan chuckled. Once again, Peter looked away and waited until they left the bus. Then he went down the aisle and got off.

And that left Josh, Andy, and me on the bus. I knew Josh would ask why I didn't sit with them, and Andy would accuse me of not wanting to sit with Peter because I wanted to make friends with the cool guys.

"You're right," I said before either of them had a chance to speak. "I didn't feel like sitting with Peter. But I didn't make friends with the cool guys either. And I don't think I'm going to."

Josh blinked with surprise. "How'd you know I was gonna ask about that?"

"Because that's what you asked me yesterday," I said.

"What are you talking about?" he said. "How could I have asked that yesterday?"

"Because we were all on this bus and you asked me why I didn't want to sit with you," I explained.

Andy and Josh shared a bewildered look.

"I've got news for you, Jake," Andy said. "You weren't here yesterday. Today's the first day of camp."

"It is for you guys," I said. "But it's the third day for me. Actually, it's my first day for the third time."

Josh and Andy traded really worried looks.

"Are you feeling okay?" Josh asked me.

"No, I'm totally freaked," I said. "This is the third time I've stood on this bus and talked to you like this. And for all I know I may be doing it for the rest of my life."

"Maybe you need to get some more sleep," Andy said, a little nervously.

"No, guys, I'm telling you the truth," I said. Then I explained how I was trapped in the first day of camp, just like I'd once been trapped in the first day of school.

Neither of my friends said a word when I was done. I could tell from their expressions that they thought I was completely insane.

"Listen, guys, I really need you to believe me," I said desperately. "When I was stuck in the first day of school I got out of it by doing the right thing. But I did the right thing yesterday and I'm still trapped."

"I think the right thing for you would be to spend the summer in a mental institution," Josh said.

"I'm not joking, guys," I said.

"Uh, boys?" Down at the front of the bus Mr. Maller had climbed back on. "Time to get off and get your bags."

"We're coming, Mr. Maller," I said.

The camp owner got off the bus.

"Who's he?" Andy asked.

"He owns the camp," I said.

"How do *you* know?" Josh asked.

"I *told* you. I've been here for three days."

Josh rolled his eyes in disbelief.

"Uh, I think we better get off," Andy said.

We started down the aisle toward the front of the bus.

"Guys," I whispered. "For the last time, you have to help me. I don't know what to do."

"It's simple, Jake," Josh whispered back. "You get off the bus. You weren't here yesterday. You were back in Jeffersonville. We spent the day Rollerblading, remember?"

"*You* guys did," I said. "Not me. I spent the day protecting Peter from the cool guys."

"Sure, Jake, whatever you say," Andy whispered.

31

We got off the bus. The driver was pulling the duffle bags out of the luggage carrier. Rick, Dan, and Zack were waiting for theirs. Peter got his duffle bag and headed toward our cabin.

Josh started to say something.

"Your cabins are over there." I pointed toward the cabins on the other side of the athletic field.

"How do you know?" Andy asked.

"I *told* you," I said wearily. "I've already been here, done this."

"We better check with a counselor just to make sure," Josh said, clearly not trusting me.

"Thanks for believing me, guys," I grumbled bitterly.

Josh had a pained expression on his face. "How are we supposed to believe that you were here yesterday when we were with you back in Jeffersonville?"

I was tired of trying to explain it. Maybe I was expecting too much from my friends. I mean, even I found it hard to believe. And I was *living* it!

I left Josh and Andy, and went to get my duffle bag. Dan started to smile. I knew what he was going to ask, of course.

"Grenades, land mines, and mortar shells," I said. "I'm a very violent person."

He scowled.

Andy and Josh got their duffle bags and spoke to the guy with the clipboard, who pointed toward their cabins on the other side of the athletic field.

Andy gave me a puzzled look.

"Believe me now?" I asked.

He didn't answer.

"Want some advice?" I asked.

Josh and Andy nodded.

"Save your snacks. You're gonna hate lunch."

32

I started toward my cabin. Up ahead I saw Peter's white shopping bag split and all his stuff spill out onto the ground. The cool guys were right behind him. My first inclination was to hurry up and help him. But on second thought I decided not to. Before I could help Peter, I had to concentrate on figuring out how to help myself get out of the mess I was in.

Just as on the previous days, the cool guys started to hassle Peter about his Water Pik. I went around them and continued lugging my duffle bag toward the cabin. But it wasn't long before the cool guys, with their lighter bags, passed me.

This time I got to the cabin about the same time as Lewis. Inside, the cool guys had already staked out the back two bunks. Lewis and I put down our duffle bags and glanced at each other. I pointed at the bunk closest to the front of the cabin.

"Want to share this one?" I asked.

Lewis nodded.

"Top or bottom?" I asked.

"I'll take the top," he said.

"You don't want to take that one, Sleeping Beauty," Zack said from his bunk in the back of the cabin. "Only the dweebs want to be close to the counselor."

"Come on back here with us," said Rick. "You can take the top of my bunk."

"No, thanks," I said, and started to unpack.

Peter was the last camper to enter the cabin. The only bed left was the top of Rick's double decker. Peter lugged his stuff toward it.

Zack turned to Rick. "Must be your lucky day," he said with a snigger.

Lewis and I glanced at each other, but said nothing.

Once again it took a while to get all my stuff unpacked. I knew I had to do something different if I wanted to get out of the first day of camp, but I still didn't know what to do. Then Marty arrived and showed us how the cabin worked. After he left for the waterfront, Zack strolled toward my bunk. Lewis was on top, tacking up his car pictures. Zack went through the small, fast car routine. Lewis told him to get lost, thereby earning the nickname of Mighty Mouse.

"So we got Mighty Mouse and Sleeping Beauty in the first bunk," Zack said, taunting us.

Lewis stuck another picture on the rafter and didn't say a word.

Zack turned to me. "Wanna play some tetherball, Sleeping Beauty?"

"No, thanks," I replied.

"What's wrong?" Zack said. "You chicken, Sleeping Beauty? Maybe we'll have to call you Sleeping Chicken."

"Or Chicken Beauty," added Dan.

"The mucous brain says, 'What?' " I said.

"What?" said Zack.

I caught Rick's eye. He smiled.

Zack put his hands on his hips. "Man, what a winner cabin we've got this year. Mighty Mouse, Sleeping Chicken, and Gummi Bear."

Following Lewis's lead, I ignored him. Zack turned to Peter and challenged him to play tetherball. When Peter admitted he didn't know what tetherball was, Zack and Dan made fun of him.

A few moments later, Peter, Dan, and Zack went outside to play. This time Rick followed, then stopped by the screen door until the others had gone outside. I was surprised to see him turn to Lewis and me.

"You guys coming?" he asked.

Lewis and I both shook our heads. Rick paused for a moment as if he wasn't certain what to do. Then he went outside.

As soon as Rick had gone, Lewis went to the

screen door and looked out. We could hear Zack and Dan laughing as Zack humiliated Peter in tetherball. Inside, Lewis just watched.

Meanwhile, I kept wondering how I was ever going to get out of the first day of camp.

33

Later we all went to the dining hall for lunch. I walked alone, a dozen yards behind Zack, Rick, and Dan. Behind me Lewis and Peter talked quietly.

Just as on the first day, I wondered what they were talking about. This time I slowed my pace and tried to eavesdrop.

"You have to stand up to them," Lewis was saying. "If you don't, they're going to make you miserable the whole time you're here."

I slowed up even more. Now I was walking with them. Peter gave me a nervous look out of the corner of his eye.

"There's one thing I don't get," I said quietly to Lewis. "When you stood up to Zack before, how'd you know he wouldn't just haul back and smash you?"

"I didn't know for sure," Lewis said. "But I figured he'd have to be really stupid to do something like that on the first day of camp. Besides, I think he's mostly talk."

Peter just listened, but didn't say anything.

Once again, Josh, Andy, and I met before lunch.

"Still think you're trapped in the first day of camp?" Josh asked.

"I don't *think* it," I said. "I *know* it."

Josh and Andy shared an uncomfortable look.

"So how's it going with the cool guys and Peter the dweeb?" Andy asked.

"They're really giving him grief," I said.

"You standing up for him?" Andy asked.

"That doesn't work," I said.

Andy and Josh gave each other another funny look.

"What do you mean?" asked Andy.

"I mean I tried it yesterday and it didn't work," I said.

"You tried what yesterday?" Josh asked.

"I protected Peter from the cool guys," I said.

"Jake, I'm really getting worried about you," Andy said. "We keep telling you that you weren't here yesterday."

"And I keep telling you I was," I said. "You think I want to spend the rest of my life trapped in the first day of camp, eating American Chop Suey for lunch every day?"

Josh wrinkled his nose. "What's American Chop Suey?"

231

"You'll know in about a minute," I said.

Both Josh and Andy were quiet for a moment. Then Josh said, "Okay, Jake, for the sake of argument, let's say you really are stuck in the first day of camp. What are Andy and I supposed to do about it?"

That was a good question.

"I don't know," I said. "But it definitely feels better knowing that someone believes me."

By now, Mr. Maller was standing at the microphone. He began his speech welcoming us to camp.

"Guess we better get back to our tables," Josh said.

"See you later, Jake." Andy said.

"One last thing," I said. "Whatever you do this afternoon, *don't* go on the nature walk."

Josh and Andy gave me bewildered looks. Then shaking their heads in puzzlement, they went back to their tables.

34

By the time I got back to my table, Peter was twisted around in his seat, listening to Mr. Maller's welcoming speech. Dan was reaching across the table and putting the plastic wrap over Peter's glass.

I locked eyes with Lewis, and we shared a knowing look. But then he looked away. I just didn't get it. If protecting Peter wasn't the right thing to do, then what was? Certainly not joining the cool guys and picking on him. What other choice was there?

Mr. Maller's speech ended. The camp waiters were coming out of the kitchen with big trays of American Chop Suey. Meanwhile, Zack reached for the metal pitcher in the middle of the table. "Who wants bug juice?"

"Me, me, me, me." Everyone at the table said they wanted some.

"Here you go." Zack stood up and poured out the bug juice. Just as he had on the first day, he held the pitcher high so that a long red stream cascaded into the glass in front of each kid.

Finally every glass except Peter's was filled.

"So, Gummi Bear, you sure you want some?" Zack asked.

Peter nodded.

I just couldn't stand the idea of him getting splattered with bug juice again. Maybe stopping Zack wasn't the right thing to do, but I had to do it anyway.

"Hey, Peter," I said. "Look at your glass."

Peter looked down at his glass. His eyes widened.

"Bombs away." Zack poured.

Peter pulled his glass away and slid his chair back to avoid getting splattered.

Splash! The red bug juice hit the table and splattered in every direction. A little of it landed on Peter, but this time more hit Marty.

"Hey!" Marty jumped up, glowering at Zack. "What'd you do that for?"

"It's not my fault Gummi Bear pulled his glass away," Zack said.

"Yeah, but look." Peter shoved the plastic-covered glass to Marty, who'd grabbed a handful of napkins and started to blot the bug juice off his shirt.

"Who put the plastic on Peter's glass?" Marty asked, looking at Zack and Dan. Neither of them answered. Marty nodded knowingly just the same.

Zack put down the pitcher and sat down looking pretty ticked.

"The bonehead says, 'What?' " I mumbled.

"What?" said Zack.

I winked at Lewis, but he just looked back at me with a blank expression.

The only person who smiled was Rick.

35

After lunch the cool guys went off to play basketball. Peter asked me if I wanted to go on the nature walk with him. I said I appreciated his asking, but I wasn't up to it.

This time I went down to the waterfront. When I got there, Lewis was standing on a dock lined with small blue sailboats. He was talking to an older guy wearing a gray counselor's T-shirt. When Lewis saw me, he waved. "Hey, Jake, got a second?"

I went over. "What's up?"

"I was thinking about taking a boat out, but they have a rule that you have to sail with a buddy," Lewis said. "Want to go?"

"I don't know how to sail," I said.

"No sweat," said Lewis. "I'll do everything."

A few minutes later I was sitting in the bow of a sailboat. Lewis was in the stern, steering with the rudder and pulling the ropes attached to the white sail overhead.

The breeze on the lake moved us along at an even pace. Not exactly thrilling, but it was relaxing.

"Thanks for coming," Lewis said.

"No prob," I said. "So you like sailing, huh?"

"Naw, I hate it." Lewis smiled a little to let me know he was kidding.

I reached over the side and dipped my hand in the lake. "Brrr, the water's cold."

"Better get used to it," Lewis said.

"Why?"

"Because first thing every morning Marty's gonna make us swim."

"First thing in the morning!?" I gasped. "Are you serious?"

Lewis nodded. "Marty's a swim instructor. I know a guy who was in his cabin last year. He said Marty always makes his cabin do it."

"Bummer," I said.

Lewis agreed. Then we talked about where Lewis learned to sail, and about the sailboat his parents shared with another family. It was sort of strange — how friendly and talkative he was on the sailboat when he was so quiet everywhere else.

"As long as I get to sail, this is gonna be a good summer," he said.

"Too bad it won't be good for Peter," I said. "Not with those dipwads picking on him all the time."

"I told him he has to stand up to them," Lewis said.

"Yeah, I know," I said. "But I'm starting to think maybe he doesn't know how."

"Maybe it doesn't matter," Lewis said with a shrug. "Maybe Zack and his friends will get bored picking on Peter and find other things to do."

From the previous days I knew that wouldn't happen. "Er, I doubt it. I think they're planning to mess him up pretty good tonight."

Lewis nodded, but didn't answer.

We sailed around the lake for a while more. There wasn't much for me to do, so I just thought about stuff.

And that's when I had the idea for helping Peter.

It was risky, but it just might work.

36

O nce again, everybody met at the cabin before dinner. Even though I hadn't played basketball that afternoon, I still decided to take a shower. When I came out of the bathroom, Zack was bugging Peter about the nature walk again.

"What are you, some kind of freak?" Zack asked.

Peter bowed his head.

"Hey, Zack . . ." Rick started to say.

"Yeah, what?" Zack snapped.

"Maybe you should leave the guy alone," Rick said.

"Guy?" Zack smirked and stared straight at Peter. "I don't see a guy. I don't know what I see. It's like something from another planet."

Rick didn't answer. He just looked at me.

"The fleabrain says, 'What?' " I muttered.

"What?" said Zack.

Rick grinned.

"Shower's free," I said.

Zack went into the bathroom. Rick and I both watched him. Then we turned and looked at each other. Whose side was he really on? I wondered.

"What happened to you guys?" I asked Josh and Andy outside the dining hall before dinner that night. They were both covered with red welts.

"We went on the nature walk," Andy said, scratching a bunch of swollen lumps on his neck.

"Are you serious?" I gasped. "That's exactly what I told you *not* to do."

"Yeah, but we had to find out why you didn't want us to do it," Josh said, scratching his arm.

"Because you'd get eaten alive by mosquitos," I said.

"We found that out," said Andy as he scratched his ear.

"So, you still think you're trapped in the first day of camp?" Josh asked.

"I don't *think* it," I said. "I *know* it."

Josh and Andy gave each other a skeptical look. Then Josh said, "Okay, listen, we had a talk. We still find this really hard to believe, Jake. But then, we never would have believed that you could get stuck in the President's body, or that Andy would switch bodies with your dog. So just in case it's true, is there anything we can do to help?"

"You guys still have your Cheese Whiz?" I asked.

After dinner we went back to the cabin. Zack and Dan talked in low voices as they planned what they were going to do to Peter later. Then Dan went into the bathroom and stayed forever. After a while, Marty got impatient and called into the bathroom to ask Dan if he was okay, and Dan called back that he'd be out in a second. Then Zack made the joke about being lost and everyone laughed.

Meanwhile, I turned to Lewis and Peter. "Why don't we wait outside?" I suggested.

As soon as Peter and Lewis came outside, I told them what the cool guys were planning to do to Peter.

"They can't sneak out during the movie," Peter said. "Marty won't let them."

"Marty won't be there to stop them," I said.

Lewis frowned. "How do you know?"

"Uh . . ." I couldn't tell him the truth. "I heard some other counselors talking. They said they were going to get together during the movie and try to figure out how to meet the counselors from the girls' camp. I have to believe Marty will be interested."

Lewis gave me a sly grin. "Yeah, well, you're probably right about that."

"If you know what Zack's planning," Peter said, "why don't you tell Marty. Then he'll talk to them."

"Talking to them won't change anything," I said.

Peter gave Lewis a questioning look.

"He's probably right," Lewis said.

Then I told them my plan. Well, not *all* of it. But most of it.

"I don't know, Jake." Peter swallowed nervously when I'd finished. "If it doesn't work, they could make us really miserable for the next month."

"I'm willing to take that risk," I said. "And if you don't try it, your life is gonna be miserable for the next month anyway. Why not give it a shot? At least this way there's a *chance* things could turn out okay."

Peter's shoulders sagged and he stared at the ground. "Maybe I should just go home. I didn't want to come to camp in the first place."

"You can't just quit," I said. "You can't run away your whole life. Just because you like different things than they do doesn't mean they're better than you and you're worse. You're just different, Peter. And you have to stand up and face them."

Peter bit his lip and glanced at Lewis, who nodded back as if he agreed with me.

Peter let out a big sigh. "Okay. Let's try it."

37

Later I sat on the bench in the back of the dining hall with Peter and Lewis. At my feet was Andy's one-million candle power SuperBeam flashlight, which I'd asked him to lend me along with the Cheese Whiz. As soon as the movie started, Marty warned us not to get into any trouble, and left. Then the cool guys disappeared.

"Ready?" I whispered to Peter and Lewis.

"I don't know," Peter whispered back nervously. "You sure this is a good idea?"

"No," I whispered. "But can you think of anything better?"

Peter shook his head.

"Then let's do it," I said.

The crickets were chirping in the moonlight. Lewis, Peter, and I snuck around the back of the cabins until we got to B-13. Inside the cabin we could hear whispers and the squeak of bedsprings as the cool guys set their booby traps.

Lewis and I opened our day packs, which we'd hidden behind the cabin before going to the dining hall to see the movie. We took out rope and the cans of Cheese Whiz. Then Lewis and Peter got out their flashlights. I was already carrying Andy's SuperBeam.

"Ready?" I whispered.

"Ready," Lewis replied.

We quietly snuck around to the front of the cabin. Inside the cool guys were still setting up their booby traps. But when the front door creaked, they looked up.

Click! Click! Click!

Lewis, Peter, and I flicked on our flashlights and aimed the beams right into their eyes. Lewis got Dan, Peter got Rick, and I got Zack with the SuperBeam. They all cowered, holding up their hands to block the bright light, squinting as they tried to see.

"Hey! What's going on?"

"Turn those things off!"

"Stop shining it in my eyes!"

We kept the flashlights on, blinding them, and didn't say a word.

"Who are you guys?" Dan asked.

I nudged Peter.

"Uh, we are the Dork Protection Posse," Peter said.

"What?"

"The Dork Protection Posse," Peter repeated.

"We protect dorks against those who seek to do them harm."

"Wait a minute." Zack straightened up. Even though the SuperBeam was still blinding him, he smiled. "I know who you are. You're Gummi Bear. And I bet your buddies are Sleeping Beauty and Mighty Mouse."

"The Dork Protection Posse, huh?" Dan said with a nasty grin.

Still shielding his eyes from the lights, Zack took a step toward us. "Isn't that cute?" he asked. "The Dork Protection Posse has come to protect the dork."

"Yeah," added Dan. "But who's gonna protect the Dork Protection Posse?"

They came toward us. Peter took a step back and glanced at me. "Now what?"

38

Zack and Dan were closing in on us. Peter, Lewis, and I backed toward the wall.

"I thought we were gonna get back up help," Peter said nervously.

"I thought so too," I said.

"So where is it?" Peter asked.

"Good question," I answered, glancing at Rick.

Dan and Zack were getting closer. We kept our flashlights on their faces, but it didn't stop them.

"This was a really great idea, Jake," Lewis muttered sarcastically.

"Hey, I only said we should try it, okay?" I shot back. "I never promised you it would work."

Meanwhile, Zack was rolling up the sleeves of his shirt. "I think the Dork Protection Posse is about to become the *Dead* Protection Posse."

"Yeah," said Dan. "Dead Meat."

They were only a few feet away now. I looked at Rick again. This time I caught his eye.

"Wait a minute, guys," Rick said.

Zack and Dan stopped. "What is it?" Zack asked.

"This is dumb," Rick said. "Somehow they found out we were playing a trick on them, so they decided to play a trick on us. I don't see why it has to turn into an all-out rumble."

"You chicken?" Zack sneered.

"No, I'm not chicken," Rick shot back. "I just don't see the point in hurting them. They didn't do anything to us."

"That's right," Zack said. "And now I'm gonna make *sure* they don't do anything to us."

It was time to make my move. I quickly muttered, "The bozo says, 'What?' "

"What?" Zack frowned.

Rick grinned.

"Come on, Rick," I said. "You know what I'm talking about."

The smile disappeared from Rick's face.

Zack stopped and looked back at Rick. "What's he talking about?"

"Peabrain says, 'What?' " I said.

"What?" Zack spun around and wrinkled his forehead.

Rick grinned again.

"It'll be four against two," I said to Rick.

"Huh?" Zack looked back and forth between us. "What's going on?"

Rick looked uncertain.

"Now I get it," Lewis whispered. "He's the back up?"

I nodded and looked at Rick. "Come on, man. This way they'll leave Peter alone and we'll all have a decent month."

"What?" said Zack.

"That's what the veghead said," I said.

Rick grinned.

"Veghead?" Zack scowled.

"Hey, I get it!" Dan gasped. "The veghead says, 'What?'"

Zack turned. "What?"

"That's what the veghead said," Dan tried to explain.

Meanwhile, the rest of us rolled our eyes and grinned.

"The . . . veghead . . . says . . . 'What?'" Zack muttered to himself. Suddenly his eyes widened. "The bozo says, 'What?' . . . The bonehead says, 'What?' . . . The peabrain says 'What?'"

He finally understood.

Zack grit his teeth, balled his hands into fists, and spun to face me. There was murder in his eyes. "Why you . . ."

I quickly looked at Rick. Now I *really* needed him. But Rick just gave me a stony stare.

39

Zack came toward me, prepared to kill. I dropped the SuperBeam and raised my fists. Next to me, Peter and Lewis did the same thing.

The only way we were going down was swinging. But against Dan and Zack we wouldn't have a chance.

"Hold it," Rick said.

Zack stopped. "Why?"

Rick walked around him and stood with Lewis, Peter, and me. "If you take on Jake, you take us all on."

Zack narrowed his eyes. "What's with you?"

"I'm just tired of you picking on people," Rick said. "You never pick on anyone who'll fight back. I think that makes you the biggest chicken of all."

Zack sputtered and snarled, he cursed at us and said a lot of nasty stuff. But Rick was right. When it was four against two, Zack didn't want to fight.

40

Later that night I stood by my bunk, speaking quietly to Rick and Lewis.

"Thanks, guys," I said. "It wouldn't have worked without you."

"I'm glad you got me to do it," Lewis said. "Otherwise, I probably would have just stuck to myself, thinking I was lucky they were picking on Peter and not me."

Rick nodded. "I know what you mean."

"Get in your bunks, guys," Marty said.

I got into bed feeling confident that I'd done the right thing. Although I was sort of disappointed that we didn't get to dangle Zack and Dan from the rafters and give them Super Cheese Whiz Wedgies.

I hadn't picked on Peter, and I hadn't protected him either. I'd helped him learn how to protect himself. That *had* to be the right thing to do. And hopefully it would be my ticket into the second day of camp, and to an okay time for the rest of the month.

Despite the lumpy pillow and itchy blanket, I slept soundly that night.

41

DAY FOUR

I felt a bump and opened my eyes. *Huh!?* What was I doing on the bus again?

We were pulling into the parking lot.

No! NO! *NO!*

Not again!

It couldn't be!

It wasn't fair!

"You can't do this to me!" I shouted angrily. "I did everything right! I did everything I possibly could! I've been *good!*"

Every head on the bus turned.

"You don't get it," I told them. "I've been here before. I've done this."

They all stared at me. A sea of frowns. They thought I was crazy.

I turned to Zack, Dan, and Rick in the back of the bus. "Zack, you're gonna pick on Peter today. You're gonna challenge him to one-handed, one-footed tetherball. You're gonna put plastic wrap on his glass so that the bug juice spills on him, and put detergent in his Water Pik. Dan, you're gonna go along with whatever Zack does because you're just a follower. Rick, you're gonna go along with Zack, too, even though you don't like it. Deep down inside you don't like picking on people, but you feel like you're stuck with Zack because it's important for you to be cool."

I turned to Lewis. "You're gonna stay out of it, Lewis. Zack's going to pick on you a little, but you're going to stand up to him."

"How do you know I have a Water Pik?" Peter asked from his seat.

"Believe me, I know," I said.

"What about Andy and me?" Josh asked.

"You guys aren't involved in this," I said. "Your cabins are on the other side of the athletic field. But hold onto your Cheeze Whiz and crackers. You're gonna need that stuff after you see what they serve for lunch."

Zack, Dan, and Rick gave me strange looks as they passed my seat and got off the bus.

Peter, Andy, and Josh were still looking at me like I'd lost my marbles.

Why was I still in the first day of camp?

What could I possibly have done wrong?

Lewis stood up and got off the bus, followed by Peter.

Now only Josh, Andy, and I were left on the

bus. They stood up and slung their day packs over their shoulders.

"Aren't you getting off?" Andy asked.

And go through all that garbage again? I shook my head.

"You have to get off the bus, Jake," Josh said.

"No way," I said. "I'm not doing this again."

"You're not doing *what* again?" Andy asked.

There was no point in explaining. They wouldn't believe me, and it made no difference anyway.

But if I didn't get off the bus, then I wouldn't have to go through the first day of camp again.

"Uh, boys?" Down at the front of the bus Mr. Maller had climbed back on. "Time to get off and get your bags."

I stayed seated. Andy and Josh gave me worried looks.

"Come on," Andy whispered urgently. "They want you off the bus."

I crossed my arms and shook my head. "No way."

"Come on, boys," Mr. Maller said. "We need this bus."

"Jake, for the last time," Josh pleaded.

"Go on," I said. "Have a great camp experience."

Josh and Andy frowned at each other, then looked back at me.

"Are you serious?" Josh asked. "We wouldn't even be here if it weren't for you."

"Yeah, this whole thing was your idea," Andy said.

"I'm sure you'll have a great time," I said.

"Boys?" Mr. Maller said. "Is something wrong?"

Josh turned to him. "Yeah, our friend Jake won't get off the bus."

The corners of Mr. Maller's mouth fell. I doubt he needed this kind of aggravation on the first day of camp. He came down the aisle toward me.

"What's your name, son?" he asked.

I told him.

"We need this bus back," he said. "You have to get off."

"Listen, Mr. Maller," I said. "I'm really sorry to do this to you, but there's no way I'm getting off this bus."

42

Mr. Maller talked to me for a long time. Then he got Marty to come talk to me.

Then they called the state police and got a trooper to come talk to me.

Then they called my parents and said they had to come get me.

Four hours later my dad got there. I was still sitting in the bus. Dad wasn't happy.

I put my duffle bag in our van and he drove me home.

"Why, Jake?" he asked on the way.

"I can't explain it, Dad," I said. "Just believe me. It has to be this way."

Dad shook his head and sighed. "Well, at least it was the first day. I can still get a refund."

We rode along in silence for a while. Then I remembered something.

"Hey, Dad, does Jessica know I'm coming home?"

"I don't see how she could," Dad replied. "She's over at the town pool, at work."

Good, I thought.

Later that afternoon I stood by the living room window and watched my sister come up the walk. Just as she reached the front door, I pulled it open.

"Ahhh!" she screeched. "Jake, what are you doing here?"

"I want my donuts," I growled.

"What!?" She stared at me in wide-eyed disbelief.

"You heard me. I want my donuts."

Her jaw dropped. "You . . . you came all the way home from camp to get your donuts?"

"Nobody takes my donuts."

"Are you crazy?"

"Just give me my donuts!"

"I . . . I can't," she stammered. "I ate them."

"Then I'm gonna *cut* them out of you." I went into the kitchen and came back with a dull butter knife.

When I got back to the front door, it was wide open. Jessica was running down the street as fast as she could.

That night I laid my head down on my nice soft feather pillow and pulled up my comfortable blanket. I couldn't remember being so glad to see my own bed.

After all, how can you be stuck in the first day of camp if you're not there?

43

DAY FIVE

I felt a bump and opened my eyes.

Oh, no! I was on the bus again.

This had to be some kind of joke.

A really bad, sick joke.

"Have a nice nap, Sleeping Beauty?" Zack asked.

Was there *nothing* I could do to get out of the first day of camp?

"What's the matter?" Zack asked. "Can't talk?"

But there *had* to be a way out. Last time it happened, when I was trapped in the first day of school, I'd figured out how to escape it.

That meant I was *still* doing something wrong.

I just had to figure out what it was.

"Hey, I'm talking to you," Zack said.

I had to think. I had to concentrate. I had to retrace my steps through the past four days. Somewhere in those days was the key, the missing link that would get me out of this mess.

"Hey," Zack said.

I looked up at him. "Bug off, wombat."

"Huh?" Zack started to make a fist.

"Lay off him," Rick said.

Zack glowered at me, but continued down the aisle and got off the bus.

Was I supposed to do something different with Peter? It didn't make sense. Somehow, deep inside, I knew that helping Peter learn to defend himself *was* the right thing to do.

But then why was I still trapped in the first day of camp? Was there *someone else* I had to help?

"Aren't you getting off?" Andy asked. He and Josh were standing with their day packs slung over their shoulders.

Did I really have to get off and go through it all again?

I guess I had to . . . until I figured out what to do.

That day I tried to do *everything* right.

I helped Peter learn to defend himself again.

I warned him about the plastic wrap.

I sailed with Lewis and got him to join the Dork Protection Posse.

I got Rick to take our side against Zack and Dan.

Finally, it was time to go to sleep.

I went into the bathroom and washed up.

I was halfway back to my bunk when I realized I'd forgotten to do something. It was something I'd forgotten to do *every* night since I'd gotten to camp.

But it couldn't be the answer, could it?

I wasn't going to take any chances.

I went back into the bathroom . . . and brushed my teeth.

44

DAY SIX

I felt a bump and opened my eyes.

I was on the bus again.

I was going through the first day of camp again!

I was going to look at American Chop Suey again!

"No! *No!*" I screamed.

I couldn't take it!

Everyone stared at me. I didn't care. I jumped out of my seat and ran to the front of the bus.

"Hey!" the driver shouted as I grabbed the wheel and jammed my foot against the gas pedal, flooring it.

Varrroooom! The bus's wheels spun wildly, spraying gravel around the parking lot. The bus lurched forward. Outside campers and counselors dove out of the way.

"Hey! What's he doing?" "Stop!" "Look out!" Inside the bus kids screamed as we hurtled over a log barrier and caromed across the grass toward the lake.

"*You're gonna kill us all!*" the bus driver shouted as we grappled over the steering wheel.

"*I don't care!*" I screamed. "*I —* "

"Hey, Jake, wake up!" Someone was shaking my shoulder. "Jake?"

I opened my eyes.

I was lying in my camp bunk. Marty, Peter, and Lewis were staring down at me. Marty's hand was on my shoulder.

"You okay?" he asked.

The sun was shining outside. The air had a fresh chilly morning smell. Despite my lumpy pillow and itchy blanket, I felt warm and cozy.

"Where am I?" I asked.

"Camp Walton," Marty said.

"What day is it?" I asked.

"The second day of camp," said Lewis.

"You must've had a bad dream," added Peter.

I sat up and rubbed my eyes.

"You okay now?" Marty asked.

"Uh . . . yeah . . . I guess." I nodded.

Was it possible?

Had I really gotten out of the first day of camp!?

Marty clapped his hands together. "Okay, guys, get your swimsuits on."

"What're you talking about?" Zack asked. "We haven't had breakfast yet."

"In this cabin we always take a nice cold swim in the lake before breakfast," Marty announced. "Come on, guys, let's go."

Everyone groaned.

I pulled my blanket up to my chin, dreading the thought of swimming in that freezing cold lake. If only I could be trapped in the first day of camp again!